THE KINGPINS OF RIVERBEND

RICHARD HALVEY

NEWMAN SPRINGS PUBLISHING
320 Broad Street
Red Bank, NJ 07701

First originally published by Newman Springs Publishing 2020

ISBN 978-1-64801-273-0 (Paperback)
ISBN 978-1-64801-274-7 (Digital)

Printed in the United States of America

To my Dad, a pin boy and a bowler.

PROLOGUE

"It's Vinnie."

I froze for a moment. I knew the voice but was unprepared to hear it. The last time I talked with Vinnie was at least twenty years ago.

"Vinnie? I used to know a Vinnie," I said. "I heard he moved to a monastery somewhere in Italy and took a vow of silence. Otherwise, I would have heard from him more than once in the last twenty years."

"Mingo's gone," he said, ignoring my swipe at him. "Dropped dead of a heart attack at the bowling alley. The police have the deep fryer in custody."

A few close friends, a slew of frustrated creditors, and three ex-wives also knew Mingo as Marcus Aurelius Pandolfo. He acquired the nickname Mingo when, at the age of seventeen, he decided to emulate the Indian sidekick from the Daniel Boone television show by attempting to throw a hatchet into the middle of the family sugar maple. It was mildly unfortunate that he connected instead with the bathroom window. It was disastrous that his unsuspecting father chose precisely that moment to try his new Gillette safety razor, nearly slicing off his chin as the small axe crashed through the glass. With the bloodied double-edged razor still in hand, he bolted into the backyard where a stunned Mingo contemplated what he assumed would be his last moments on earth. As his father took a step toward him, Mingo turned and began running. His pursuing father exhorted his five-foot-six-inch, two-hundred-forty-pound body forward, and…

The race ended almost as soon as it started when Mr. Pandolfo collapsed, either from excessive blood loss or total muscle failure.

Showing uncharacteristic good sense, Mingo kept going, assuming his father was faking in order to draw him back.

Three hours and sixteen stitches later, Mr. Pandolfo returned home, went to the bathroom to recover the hatchet, marched to Mingo's room, and proceeded to bury the axe in the middle of the door. As far as anyone knew, it was never removed. Mingo obviously survived the incident, although having to sleep every night in a room with a hatchet in the door probably helped turn him into the tormenting human being we knew.

When Mingo's older brother heard the story, he said, "You thought you were Ed Ames? Nice going, Mingo." The name stuck. Of course, it didn't hurt that Mingo inherited his father's chiseled beak and his mother's jet black hair, wearing it collar length, pushed straight back, and pompadour high in an effort to add three inches to a height he also inherited from his father.

"I'm sorry to hear that," I said. I was at least sure I was sorry for the people in the hereafter who had to put up with him for eternity. "Is Kelley taking care of the arrangements?"

"Of course," Vinnie said.

"I'll send flowers, I guess. You think it would be okay to say 'Rest in peace, Mingo'? He's still Mingo, right?"

"Yeah," Vinnie said. "Once everybody forgot about Ed Ames, he became proud of the name. He used to tell his wives Mingo was the Italian god of sex. He forgot to add, by yourself."

"So what are you not telling me? Jesus, Vinnie, I don't hear from you for twenty years, and out of the blue, you decide to call me to tell me Mingo's dead. That would be the Mingo who made the summer of 1968 our personal purgatory?"

"I almost called you six years ago, but I got busy doing something," he said. "Listen G, Mingo's older brother didn't think he'd get through to you so he asked me to give you a call.

"Mingo left a request that you do his eulogy. He wanted to go out with…class. He really thought the world of you, you know."

"What am I supposed to say?" I asked. "You know how some guys get the brains and some guys get the looks and some guys get the personality. Well, Mingo got none of those."

"He was a helluva bowler," Vinnie said. "And he beat P. G. Peckham. Sort of."

He was right. As a friend, breadwinner, and husband, Mingo was a miserable failure. But as a bowler, he was an artist. An anonymous genius composing with a hard rubber ball on a laminated wood canvas.

"I'll do it," I said. "I suppose I owe him that for what happened that night. You won't be too busy to pick me up at the airport later tonight, will you?"

"Be my privilege, G."

"Good. I'll call you later with the details. We can catch up then."

Tomorrow I would be back in Riverbend.

CHAPTER 1

Everybody remembers his first job. Mine was a pin boy at Riverbend Alleys, Riverbend, New York. It was 1968, and I was thirteen years old.

I was born at Most Precious Blood Hospital on the first of June 1955. Six days later, at Most Precious Blood Church, I was christened Gianni Petrosino—Johnny with a G. I eventually gave up trying to explain how Johnny could be spelled with a G and took to introducing myself simply as G.

I had an unspectacular, routine childhood. We ate spaghetti and meatballs four times a week. My mother endured her biennial pregnancies with great patience. My father worked as a tailor. He drank dark purple wine that came in unmarked bottles of various size and shape using little juice glasses, read the local newspaper, the *Riverbend Daily Current*, from front to back, and fell asleep by nine every evening. The entire Petrosino clan was encouraged to love baseball as long as it was the Yankees. We went to church every Sunday at eleven. My mother and the growing brood occupied a short pew near the back of the church. My father would occasionally join us, depending on the weather and who was saying the mass. Mostly, he liked to stand outside with the other Italian men deciding which politician or baseball player was "a no-good piece of-a crap" this week. Of course, they only used the word crap if there were women or children within earshot. More than occasionally did we hear the word *merda* or its more common English translation. One could identify the most heinous offenders by their elevation from simple crap to dog crap, as in "that Ralph Terry is a piece of-a dog crap for giving that Polish piece of-a dog crap a home-a run in the World Series."

I was an extraordinary student at Most Precious Blood Institute. That encouraged my grandmother to let everybody know I was going to be a "big-a shot" someday.

"This is my grandson Gianni," she would say. "He's gonna be some big-a shot someday."

I thought girls were weird, dirt was good, and snakes and bugs were overrated as boyish interests. I thought reading was fun, although I was smart enough not to share that opinion with my friends. I was a decent athlete, never the star but always one of the first two or three picked. I was neither extraordinarily happy nor pitifully sad. Mostly, I remember thinking that adulthood couldn't come quickly enough. I didn't want to be a kid any longer than was absolutely necessary.

If you never heard of Riverbend, it is not surprising. In 1968, Riverbend was a town that lived only to finish dying. Fifty years earlier, it had been a thriving industrial center with a population almost as large as Albany. Within its boundaries, at the height of its prosperity, there were thirty-one churches, two excellent hospitals, five national banks, one savings and loan, a large orphanage, fifteen public schools, five Roman Catholic schools, a Carnegie library, and a post office that was an exact third scale replica of the post office building in New York City. It had a variety of textile, knitted good, grist mills, and other manufacturing operations, but what it was best known for was brooms. The City of Riverbend made more corn brooms than the rest of the United States combined, turning out twenty brooms for every minute of every day of the year.

Riverbend was so identified with brooms that the high school teams were nicknamed the Sweepers (leading to such headlines as "Sweepers Clean Up in Albany Doubleheader" and "Sweepers Whisk Hudson").

Riverbend was about halfway between Albany and Utica in a valley bisected by the Mohawk River and surrounded by thick forests of pine and hickory and ash where Indians and fur traders peacefully conducted commerce in the time before the Revolutionary War. The first white settlers were the Dutch in the mid 1600s, making their way West from Albany through the Mohawk River Valley. They named the area Broeck Camp, mainly because it was in a particularly rocky and steep area, with few permanent residents. Just a place to stop on the way upriver. The Mohawks controlled the area, having pushed the Algonquians across the Hudson, and while the Indians could be unpredictable, they generally allowed the Dutch traders to harvest the pelts that were valuable in Europe. There was plenty for everyone. The trappers didn't bother the Indians; the Indians didn't bother the trappers.

Settlement was slow and the population sparse through much of the 1700s. The harsh geography had one good effect—both armies avoided the area during the Revolutionary War and that part of the Mohawk Valley emerged relatively unscathed. In 1813, there were finally enough people and buildings to officially become a village, although only the north side of the Mohawk was originally included in the village limits. They chose the name Riverbend in recognition of the sight travelers on the river saw as they came around the turn just before the village.

Eventually, all the land on the south side was annexed. Business boomed when the Mohawk River was chosen as the route of the Erie Canal, and although the river dropped close to four hundred feet between Utica and the Hudson in Albany, an ingenious series of locks enabled barges to navigate the river. The railroads quickly followed, as did two highways for wagon traffic.

Riverbend had been settled in great numbers by the industrious immigrants of the latter nineteenth century, with each group eventually staking out its own territory. The Irish were the first to arrive, choosing the west end of town where the valley was widest for their houses but building factories wall to wall along the three miles of the Ohneka Creek. The creek dropped three hundred feet in the three miles it ran from the north border of the village to the Mohawk River, providing cheap power and a convenient waste disposal stream. They set up the first grist mills, textile plants, and small factories to make steel springs for cartage vehicles. It was a perfect location for shipping goods to Albany and to feed the voracious appetites of New York City. The Irish were followed quickly by the Italians who settled the low area in the east end and established large vegetable gardens and dairy farms on the fertile land across the river on what was called the South Side. The Italians found niches as tailors and barbers and shoemakers, grocers and druggists. Last came the wave of eastern Europeans, the Slavs, Poles, and Ukrainians, who formed the pool of labor needed to keep the factories belching the smoke that covered the valley in a pallor of prosperity. They settled on the hills on the northeast part of the valley, closest to the factories, the area known to all as Slav Hill. The factory owners and wealthy merchants eventually built enormous houses in the northwest part of the city, far above and away from the smell of the effluent of people and factories.

By 1885, Riverbend had grown enough to incorporate as a city and was far more prosperous than many of the surrounding cities. At its height, Riverbend could claim forty thousand residents. Circuses, great boxing matches, baseball games, or horse races would be held on the weekends. Life in Riverbend was grand, and there was hardly a resident who didn't enjoy the fruits of Riverbend's prosperity. During World War II, the factories along the Ohneka hummed through three shifts. That all changed after the war. In the 1950s, the factories that had employed so many skilled workers began an amazingly rapid exodus.

By 1968, almost all the factories had moved to some foreign country or the south where labor was cheaper and unions were absent. Riverbend was left with the hulking carcasses of empty brick four-story buildings and twenty-two thousand people still clinging to the hope that the town could once again be the center of something.

The one thing Riverbend still had was a picture post-card setting, at least from a distance. From the top of Wortham Hill where the Wortham Broom Company family once lived, the Mohawk appeared to flow lazily to the Hudson, its smooth, gleaming surface belying the agitated currents that churned underneath and hiding the sewage and factory waste that had been deposited there for the better part of a century. Along its main street, a hundred yards from the Mohawk, were cautiously designed buildings from the 1800s that housed the merchants who were either too stubborn or too embedded to leave.

At the eastern edge of the commercial downtown, behind the storefronts, on an isolated triangle of dirt was a small, gray brick building with grimy windows and a painted wooden sign over the door that read.

Riverbend Alleys
Riverbend, NY

Since it was not on a street, it had no street address, but the little mail addressed to Riverbend Alleys, Riverbend, New York, always found its way there. On July 1, 1968, in the summer, thirteen years after I was born, I walked into Riverbend Alleys to ask for a job.

CHAPTER 2

I opened the door and was nearly flattened by the smell. A toxic wave of stale cigarettes and DiNobilis, those crumpled black, wine-soaked Italian stogies, constituted the first sensory assault, immediately causing my eyes to water and my throat to palpitate. That was quickly followed by the enveloping odor of…bananas. Strong, sweet, overripe bananas. I looked through the heavy air for Vinnie. Naturally, it was his idea that we should become pin boys. Of course, at thirteen years old, our job potential was essentially limited to pin boy and paper boy, and Vinnie had already decided paper boy was not his style.

"Besides that, G," he told me, "my father says the *Riverbend Daily Current* is run by communists. Card-carrying pinkos. No way I can deliver newspapers for communists."

Vinnie's father owned an excavating company, Peter Antonioni and Sons, consisting of a 1940s vintage dump truck, a backhoe, and three older sons each about the size of the backhoe.

He long ago decided that anyone not engaged in manual labor probably had some connection to the communists.

"I never saw anyone who made a living with a shovel get testimonied by that McCarther guy," he once said. "They were all writers and actors. That's who the commies target. People too lazy to make an honest living and people educated beyond their intelligence."

The one exception to the manual labor rule was politicians. While he didn't trust them, he conceded someone had to take care of the business of shepherding contracts to friends and making sure the communists paid their taxes.

"Even the *putannas* deserve to make a living, G," Mr. Antonioni once told me. "They're doing the best they can with what little talent the good Lord gave them."

In a strange coincidence, at 11:00 p.m. on May 31, 1955, the pregnant Maria Antonioni found herself in a semi-private room at Most Precious Blood Hospital with an equally pregnant Contessa Petrosino.

"Is this your first one, dear?" Maria asked.

"Yes," said Contessa. "How many children do you have?"

"God has seen fit to bless me with three strong, beautiful sons," Maria said. "And now he has blessed me again with this child."

"When God blesses you, do you feel like throwing up?" Contessa said.

"It wouldn't surprise me," Maria said.

Four hours later, Maria Antonioni delivered a healthy baby boy. One hour after that, Contessa Petrosino did the same.

In the waiting room, a petrified Tommy Petrosino and a sleepy Peter Antonioni shook hands for the first time and exchanged DiNobilis in wrappers that said, "*È ragazzo.*"

"It's good that your first child is a boy. Then you don't feel so much pressure to make another one right away," Peter said. "I am forty-nine years old, and my wife, Maria, is forty-four. God gave us three sons and then made us wait sixteen years for another. He is a mysterious but charitable God. I think I'll name my fourth son Vincenzo, after the patron saint of Catholic charity."

Tommy Petrosino hardly heard a word. "My son will be Gianni," he said. "It is my father's name."

From that point, Vinnie and I were connected, as if we were twins. He was my best friend, and I his, in every sense of the term.

Vinnie Antonioni was at once the most impish and charming child in the east end. He would never be more than a slightly above-average student through high school, more for lack of effort than lack of ability, but he did have two undeniable skills. First, when it came to dealing with people, Vinnie was a natural. As soon as he was old enough to wander away from his house on his own, Vinnie undertook the task of ingratiating himself to every Italian woman on his block.

"Those groceries look heavy, Mrs. Girardi," he said. "Can I help you bring them upstairs?"

"Why thank you, Vincenzo," she said. "And perhaps I might find some *sfogliatelli* and milk for you."

"Oh, you don't have to do that, Mrs. G," he said, "unless it would be an insult for me to refuse."

Second, he had a savant's ability to remember all kinds of statistics. Batting averages, state populations, and as it turns out, bets on the daily number. In the days before states decided gambling was only immoral and illegal if someone else was running it, daily lotteries were run through a network of neighborhood luncheonettes, drug stores, barber shops, and candy stores. People would stop by daily to bet dimes and quarters and dollars on a three-digit number, which, when hit, paid off at the seemingly astronomical sum of 640-1. I was never quite sure how they figured out what the number was, but everyone seemed satisfied that the game was being run fairly.

At the end of each day, the collection people brought bags of change and betting slips to Paulie DiMeo's corner store, where they were comingled with change and slips from miles around. As everyone knew, Paulie was the biggest bookmaker in the valley. He obviously wasn't the most attentive storekeeper.

As you walked into the store, on the left were two chest-high glass cases which normally didn't have more than a Clark Bar with a faded wrapper and two packs of Blackjack gum. Behind the glass cases on shelves attached to the wall was a full stock of cigarettes, cigars, and tobacco products. On the right were empty racks designed to hold potato chips and pretzels.

Straight back was an old-style soda machine, the kind that had a lid that opened up and delivered ten ounce bottles that slid out through metal rails. Soda cost a nickel, and the machine was also fully stocked. Next to the soda machine was a large door that looked like it had been borrowed from a meat freezer. As we found out some time later, behind that door was the card room.

We were nine years old when Vinnie decided we should visit Paulie's store. "C'mon, G," he said, "let's go get a soda down at Paulie's."

"You know we can't go into Paulie's," I said. "Our fathers would kill us."

"Don't be such a chicken," he said. "We're just gonna get a soda. Who else has Coke for a nickel?"

"I don't know, Vinnie," I said. "I'm already in trouble for being late for dinner on Sunday."

"Well, I'm going," Vinnie said. "I need a soda, and why should I pay more than a nickel if I don't have to." He started walking away.

"Wait up," I said.

Vinnie naturally went in first with me following. Sitting on a stool behind the glass cases was an immense man we all knew as Tony Sharp. When Tony was a boy, his father regularly said, "You're not too sharp, are you, Tony."

Tony replied, "I am too. I'm Tony Sharp."

Aside from having an enormous girth, Tony had some problem with his right eye which caused it to appear perpetually squinting. Sitting on the stool, he looked like a bulbous version of Popeye.

"You kids can't come in here," Tony said.

"Why not?" demanded Vinnie.

"Cause kids aren't allowed, that's why not," said Tony.

"We just want a soda, that's all," said Vinnie. "Ain't our money any good here?"

Tony looked more perplexed than usual. He wasn't going to climb off his stool just to chase a couple of brats away, but that one kid didn't look like he was going to cooperate otherwise. At that moment, Paulie came through the meat locker door.

"What's going on here, Tony?" he asked.

"These kids came in here, and I told them they hadda go 'cause we don't allow kids."

Paulie looked at us, Vinnie looking thirsty and innocent and me praying he didn't decide to take us in back to the meat locker. Paulie was no more than five foot two, skinny as a stick, with thick white hair neatly brush cut about an inch high, but he looked tougher than round steak from the Acme.

"We want a soda," Vinnie said, "and we each got a nickel to pay."

"I know you two," Paulie said. "You're Antonioni's kid, and you're they one they call G."

"So if you know us," Vinnie said, "can we have a soda now."

"Tell you what, Antonioni," Paulie said, "I'll give you both a soda for free today, but you can't come back no more. Is that a deal?"

"I'll have to think about that," Vinnie said.

Every day for the next two weeks, Vinnie stopped in for a soda. One day, he stopped in and told Paulie, "Here is a quarter from Mr. Rinaldi and a dollar from Mrs. Isabel. They said the usual." Paulie took the money and walked back to the meat locker.

Within a month, Vinnie was running for most of the neighborhood. He would stop at Paulie's at the end of the day, and with no help from written betting sheets, he would rattle off names, amounts, and numbers for the day. Vinnie was invincible.

One day, a man stopped by to see Paulie while Vinnie was in the store. "I come to collect," he said. Paulie looked up at him and said, "the number was 961 yesterday. You played 916."

"The kid got it wrong," the man said.

"What do you say, Vinnie," Paulie asked.

Vinnie rattled off every number and every bet the man had made for the last two weeks. "And he never bet no 961, Paulie," Vinnie said.

"Kid says you never bet 961, then you never bet 961," Paulie said. "Now get out of here before I make sure you never bet another number anywhere ever again."

For three years, Vinnie ran numbers to Paulie until one day his father said, "Vinnie, I know you been running for Paulie. You gotta stop. You're old enough to earn a living they way Antonioni's are supposed to. With their hands."

"But, Pop," he said, "I'm doing great with Paulie."

"I didn't ask for your opinion on this," his father said. "It's time for you to learn real work."

I turned around just as Vinnie came through the door of the bowling alley. "C'mon, G. We're gonna be pin boys."

CHAPTER 3

Patrick Michael McDermott woke up one morning and realized he was as alone in the world as a thirteen-year-old could be. He was cold and hungry and exhausted after spending the last two days running from the workhouse where he had lived for as long as he could remember. He picked himself off the cobblestone that substituted for a bed, looked around, and began to sniff the air. He picked up the odor of sweet breads and followed it until he found the source. He stood outside the bakery, under the small wooden sign that displayed the shop's name, until the man inside noticed him.

The man unlocked the door, looked out at the dirty, homeless Patrick Michael McDermott, and said, "Get the feck outta here, ya miserable little urchin."

Patrick stared at him, tired and lacking options.

"Are ya deef?" the man said. "Move along before I swat yer arse."

"If I sweep yer store, will you give me some bread?" Patrick asked.

The man heaved his chest once and contemplated the boy. "Come in ya little shite," the man said, "before ya let all the heat inta the street. There's a broom in the corner. But if ya want that bread, I better not see a speck 'o dust left behind."

Patrick retrieved the broom, looked at it, and asked the man, "Do ya not have a proper broom to sweep with? I'll be lucky to move any dirt with this thing."

The man laughed and said, "Why that broom was St. Paddy's broom that he used to sweep all the snakes out of Ireland. If it worked for St. Paddy, it'll work for you. Now get to yer work so I can get to mine."

When Patrick was done and the bread was eaten, he asked the man how to get to the harbor.

"The harbor?" the man said. "Gonna be a ship captain, are ya?"

"No, sir," said Patrick. "I'll be goin' to America where a man doesn't have to be anyone to be rich and famous."

The man turned and wrapped some bread in paper, throwing in a large hunk of the cheese he thought he might have eaten for his breakfast. He handed it to the boy and said, "Here. It's a long trip from Ireland to America. You'll need something more than your brassy personality to survive that trip. Folla the Bremerton Road west. You'll find the harbor at the end of the road."

Patrick nodded at the man. "If yer ever in America, find a big house on top of a hill overlookin' a river. That'll be my place."

The man roared with laughter. "Outta here, ya daft little bastard." Patrick left. The man said to himself, "Big house on a hill by the river." Then he went to the storeroom for another sack of flour.

It was eight weeks before Patrick landed in America. He stayed in New York City for a while but found it loud and smelly and not nearly green enough. He found work on a steamer that shuttled serious men in tailored wool suits with starched white shirts and shiny silk ties between New York and Albany. One extraordinarily hot day in August, he packed all he owned in a cloth satchel, stepped off the steamer after it docked in Albany, and started walking west along the Erie Canal. West, he thought, had always been a good direction for him.

He walked for six days and then one more before finding himself on the banks of the Mohawk River in front of a painted wooden sign that read:

Village of Riverbend, NY
Founded 1813
Population 8,423

He walked north and west up the steep hills that ascended stair-like from the valley floor until he found the place. On the top of a hill overlooking the river, Patrick Michael McDermott decided he was home.

He found a room in the west end and a job at the grist mill where he toiled for twelve hours a day, six days a week. After work, he would gather discarded cornstalks from the pile behind the mill and, in his room at night, bundle them into sweep brooms of all sizes. He took them to Watson's Mercantile each Thursday evening where they sold almost as quickly as they were displayed.

One Thursday evening, Watson said to Patrick, "I need more brooms. You deliver them on Thursday, and they're gone by Saturday."

"I'm hardly sleepin' now, what between work and broom buildin'. Besides, the mill is thinkin' they should get a cut because I'm usin' what they decided are their cornstalks, even though they were gonna burn them anyway," Patrick said.

"Just bring me more brooms. They're the only ones people want, you know," Watson said. "By the way. Your brooms need a company name. I can't very well tell people they're made by some poor Irish lad in his boarding room at night, can I?"

Patrick thought a moment. He thought of the baker who gave him bread. What was the name on the sign over his head? "Tell people they are handcrafted by the Wortham Broom Company."

In 1884, when Patrick Mc Dermott was twenty-four years old, the first Wortham Broom Company factory opened on Forge Street in Riverbend, expanding three times in five years until it was the largest employer in the valley. Within a year, Patrick married a pretty girl named Jane Murphy, throwing a wedding reception that lasted three days and during which no brooms at all were made in Riverbend. They had a half dozen impossibly clever children and lived in a large house overlooking the river on the top of the hill he stood on when he first came to Riverbend.

On a cold day in the winter of 1895, Jane McDermott said to her husband, "I would like to try tenpins, but there are no places a proper woman can go. The only places to bowl are taverns where gruff men smoke, drink whiskey and beer, and fight each other for no reason."

"Tenpins for women," said Patrick. "What a marvelous idea."

In the spring of 1896, the first brick was placed on the foundation of Riverbend Alleys.

By September of that year, Jane McDermott rolled the first ball down lane number three, missing all the pins and laughing at the result. "It's perfect, Patrick," she said.

CHAPTER 4

"The owner's name is Frank," Vinnie said. "No last name. Just Frank. That's him in the small office in the corner."

The man in the corner office was cadaverously thin, with cheeks that sunk deeply into the sides of his face. He was under six feet tall, but his slimness gave him the illusion of height. He had thinning, wispy black hair that was combed straight back and plastered in place with Vitalis. He wore small wire-rimmed glasses, the sort favored by accountants. His mouth was rarely without a smoldering Lucky Strike. He sat at a small table where a copy of the *New York Daily News* lay open. Not the emaciated upstate copy, but the full New York City version with all the ads and classifieds.

Vinnie walked up to the office, and I followed close behind. Frank looked up as Vinnie entered the small room.

"My name is Vinnie Antonioni," he said, "and this is G. Gianni Petrosino. We want to be pin boys."

Frank took a shallow drag on the Lucky Strike, removed his glasses, and rubbed his eyes. "You ever been pin boys before?" he asked.

Vinnie gave Frank a puzzled look. "No... Riverbend Alleys is the only bowling place that uses them. This would actually be our first official job."

"How old are you?" Frank asked.

"We've been thirteen for most of a month now," I said.

Frank took a deeper drag on the Lucky Strike. "See that counter next to the door," he said. "Tell the guy behind the counter you're the new pin boys. He'll tell you everything you need to know."

Vinnie and I left the office. "That was a little too easy," I said. "What's the catch?"

"No catch," said Vinnie. "He just recognized us for the talents we are."

We walked over to the counter where a lanky man with lava-colored hair was sprinkling some sort of powder into red, tan, and green shoes with prominent numbers embossed on the back of the heel.

"Keeps the fungus away," he said. "What can I do for you?"

Vinnie answered him. "We're the new pin boys. I'm Vinnie, and this is G. Frank sent us over here and said you'd take care of us."

"Your timing was good, boys," he said. "We just lost two pin boys Saturday night. Mingo got pissed off and threw a ball down the lane before one of them had finished setting the pins. The boy tried to jump out of the way, but Mingo hit the pins solid and sent them flying. Broke the kid's leg. The other boy was on the next lane over watching the whole thing. One of the flying pins caught him in the head and knocked him cold. Had to call the ambulance to take him to Most Precious Blood, which there was a lot of all over the place. I guess they x-rayed his head but didn't find nothin'. He just called and said he ain't coming back. First lesson of being a pin boy—pay attention. My name's Mike, by the way, but everyone calls me Yakky. My grandmother gave me that name. Said I was the yakkiest kid she ever knew. I guess I just got a lot to say. I pretty much take care of things day to day around here. Frank just sits in the office, smokes Luckys, and reads that newspaper all day. I don't know how he can do it. Ten in the morning to ten at night reading the same newspaper. You'd think maybe he'd read a couple of papers during the day, but it's just that one *Daily News*. Hell, the paper's half pictures. He must read all the classifieds and the department store ads; otherwise, you could finish the whole thing in about an hour. Either that or he's the slowest reader on the earth. Good to have you aboard, fellas." Yakky paused momentarily to take a breath, then continued.

"Lemme give you boys the rundown on Riverbend Alleys. This building was built in 1896 by the guy who owned the old Wortham Broom Company. You musta seen the place a million times. It's one a them empty old factory buildings up on Church Street, which used to be Forge Street. His name wasn't Wortham, but I don't remember what it was exactly. He built it so his wife could bowl. You see, back then, if you wanted to bowl you found a tavern with one or two lanes, but those were rugged places and not fit for women. He decided on six lanes, same number as children he had. Painted the whole place inside a powder blue 'cause his wife said blue made people feel calmer and more like having fun. They used to bowl every Sunday afternoon after High Mass at Most Precious Blood. Just walked the block and a half, unless it was raining or snowing, in which case they had a carriage bring them over. After bowling, his wife would take the kids and oversee preparation of the Sunday dinner. Meanwhile, for three hours after that on Sunday afternoon, he'd open up the alleys to anybody who worked at the broom factory. For free. Said it wouldn't be holy to charge for sport on Sunday. After bowling, he'd give everyone a root beer and tell them he'd see 'em bright and early Monday."

I was fascinated. Vinnie looked like someone was hitting him on the head with a newspaper.

Yakky continued. "Eventually, he opened up the lanes to the public with the provisions that no one could drink hard liquor, smoke anything foul smelling, or curse unnecessarily. Back at the turn of the century, Riverbend Alleys was about as popular a hang out as there was. 'Course back then, there wasn't no movie theaters and the like. Boys and girls met for dates right here on Friday and Saturday nights. The old men would bowl in the afternoons. Evenings during the week were reserved for the factory leagues. There were some pretty good bowlers here too. Sundays were still always for the broom factory crowd. You ever heard of Jack Nickelby?"

"No," we both echoed.

"Best bowler in this area in the thirties. Became a first rate pro too. And he got his start right here," said Yakky.

"In the forties, the Wortham Broom Company started experiencing some hard times. New electric vacuum sweepers were all the rage, and although people always needed brooms, they just stopped caring about real cornstalks and handcrafting and the like. Eventually, the family sold the bowling alley to some guy who thought he might turn it into a furniture store, but he had a son killed in the war and just seemed to give up on the idea. The place stayed closed for ten years until Frank here bought it for $4,000. He didn't make no improvements really, except to paint the inside red, green, and tan and smooth out the lanes.

"We don't get the crowds here like we used to. In the 1950s, the automatic pinsetters you see at the big bowling centers became affordable, and pretty much everybody installed them. They built places that had twenty and thirty lanes with one mechanic to maintain 'em all. I heard there's even a place in Albany they're thinking about building with fifty bowling lanes. Now, if you ask me, there's no mechanical pin setting machine that can do the job that a good pin boy can, but that's the future. Everything mechanical. Pretty soon they're gonna have robots and things to take your kids to the park and clean your house. Cheap as pin boys are, it's cheaper to have them machines. And more reliable too, they think. What did you guys say your names were?" he asked.

"Vinnie and G," I said. "I'm G."

"G. What's that stand for?"

"It's short for Gianni," I said.

"Don't you spell Johnny with a J?" he asked. "Well, never mind. Vinnie and G it is. All right, let me give you the rundown on things. We got three jobs around here. Pin boy, foul spotter, and counter man. I'm the counter man, and that's not gonna change. Foul spotter is only used for the Pro League and tournaments. The rest of the time, you get to be a pin boy. There's six lanes and six pin boys on a given day. When we have to use a foul spotter and all the lanes are full, one of the pin boys has to pull a double. That means set two lanes. I decide who the foul spotter is and who gets the double. You get ten cents a line whether you're setting or spotting. Line is a game, in case you didn't know. You get here at ten in the morning every day except Sunday and Monday. The front door will be open. Frank will make sure of that. Sunday we're closed. Frank don't spend no time at church, but he don't think anyone should be paying to bowl on the Lord's day either. Same as when it was the Wortham lanes. Monday you don't have to be here until eleven. Saturday night we stay late to clean up since we ain't here on Sunday, so there's no clean up Monday morning. The first two hours, we oil the lanes and clean the place from the night before. Tuesday and Thursday nights are the Pro Leagues. We give the lanes an extra dressing of oil right before they start on those days. Last bowlers are expected to finish by ten at night, except on Saturdays when we might stay open a little late. You better bring food with you or have your mothers stop by with something. Frank don't feed the help. You work out when you eat or take a break with the other pin boys. But let me warn you. We get busy and you might not even be able to take care of business, if you know what I mean. You get one missed day of work, no questions asked. You miss two days and you're finished. Everybody gets one day off every week besides Sunday. That's based on seniority. Guy who's been here the longest gets first pick. Lots of times in the afternoons, it ain't too busy, and you might get a few extra hours off. But every night is real busy. You got any questions?"

Vinnie and I shook our heads.

"Lucky you guys are Italians. Frank don't hire nobody but Italians. He only made one exception, but you'll find out about that later. Me, I'm only half, but it's on my father's side, so I got an Italian last name. If he ever found out my mother was a Pulaski, I'd be cooked. Okay, then. Let's meet the guys and get you trained. First customers should be here in about an hour. Oh, and one other thing. No matter what, you gotta promise to stick it out for two weeks. If you can't deal with it after that, you can quit. But you gotta hang in there for two weeks. Deal?"

Vinnie said, "You don't have to worry about us, Yakky. We ain't met the job too tough for us."

CHAPTER 5

"Danny, Albert, Borneo, Crackers," Yakky yelled, "c'mere and meet the new guys." Yakky turned to us and said, "These are regular Monday guys. Charlie Horse is the pin boy who has Mondays off. Lucky you two showed up or there wouldn't have been any days off for anyone. Oh yeah, that reminds me. Make sure I get your phone numbers in case I gotta call you in on your day off."

They all stopped working and walked toward us. Yakky couldn't help himself and did the introductions.

Yakky introduced the first one to arrive as Danny. "Danny's the fastest pinsetter you ever saw. He can grab three kingpins in each hand and handle them up like they were clothespins. Natural born pin boy, he is."

Danny said, "I got a new watch. It's a real genuine Timex. It's twenty-five after eleven right now."

Danny was a boy in a man's body. Today, there are all kinds of gentle terms for people like Danny. In 1968, Danny was simply described as retarded.

"I can't tell you the time again until the big hand is on the six," Danny said. "Then it will be eleven thirty."

He had a blocky look, almost like he had been constructed from interlocking paving stones. He was clean shaven but with the beginnings of a five o'clock shadow, even at twenty-five after eleven in the morning. I recognized his haircut as being from Sal's barbershop. Sal only cut hair one way, no matter how detailed the instructions you gave him were. Clippers as close to the scalp as possible around the ears and above the neck and a half inch of hair on top of the head. Danny's eyes were the color of milk chocolate, and he looked directly at everyone he talked to. His hair was a matching color, with gray flecks sprinkled lightly throughout. He didn't have so much a smile as a grin, and it was present whenever he wasn't setting pins. That he took very seriously.

"This is Albert," said Yakky. Albert was obviously middle-aged, but it was hard to tell exactly how old he was. His face was leathery and deeply etched, and his deep blue eyes were half-closed, like he had fallen into a permanent squint. He was tall standing next to the other pin boys, but he would have been tall standing next to almost anyone. He was rail thin, except for a slightly protruding stomach, and slightly bald. Albert produced a crooked smile and nodded at the two boys.

"And this is Borneo. And say hello to Crackers." We both knew Crackers from Most Precious Blood School. He was our age, husky in a way that would eventually turn him into an overweight adult. We both nodded at him.

"I'm sure you'll get to know them real well in the next couple of weeks. Borneo will take you back and show you how to set pins. You boys have any questions, just stop by to see me. When you have a minute that is."

Borneo gave them a look of nonchalance. "Follow me," he said, "and watch the alleys. They've just been oiled."

Borneo moved nimbly on the narrow flat space between the alley gutters, and we tentatively mimicked his footsteps until we were in front of where the pins would be. "Bend low, boys," Borneo said, and he crawled through the small space at the end of the lane. "This is the cave. Get used to it because you'll be spending a lot of time back here."

Vinnie and I looked at each other. We were standing in a pit where the pins would gather after being assaulted by the ball. Above the pit was a small flat area and, slightly above that, two planks that ran the length of the space. The cave was lit by three bare lightbulbs, making it an eerie, shadowy place. It was not clear if it had been swept since the Eisenhower administration.

Vinnie said, "You think Wortham could have left a few brooms."

Borneo ignored him and started talking. "See this thing that looks like a pedal? It's called a treadle. You step on it, and it turns a wheel that pushes ten metal pegs up through the holes in the lane. That tells you exactly where to set the pins. The bottom of the pin fits just perfect over the peg. You gotta step hard on the treadle so it locks, and you better make sure it locks the first time. Time is money, boys. Now watch how I do this. Danny, grab me a couple of boxes of kingpins out of the bin." Danny opened what looked like a trap door in back of the pit, put tenpins in a cardboard box, and passed the box to Borneo. Borneo grabbed two pins with each hand and turned to show us how to hold them. "Start like this," he said. "Once you get good you can try three pins. But if you fumble them, you look like a dope. So work your way up to it. When you stand behind the lane, it should be even with your belt. You guys are kinda short, so you're gonna have to stand on a box or something. Lean over the lane and slide a little forward on your stomach, like this."

Borneo reached out and deftly placed the head pin and three pin with his left hand and, simultaneously, the two and four with the right hand. Then he snatched two more pins from the box and placed them on the pegs that identified the five and six pins. He grabbed the final four pins and, while standing, quickly set the seven, eight, nine, and ten pins. The last thing he did was release the treadle.

"Got it?" said Borneo. We both nodded because it seemed like the only thing to do. "Okay. Last thing. Once the pins are set, get out from behind the lane. When the bowlers see the pins are ready, they're likely to start rolling. See those two planks up there? Hop up there, take a seat, and wait until the pins crash. Roll the ball back, clear the downed bowling pins, and get back up on the planks. After the second ball, reset the whole ten."

"What happens if we accidently knock a pin over when we're clearing them?" I asked.

"That's easy," said Borneo. "First, it's always a good idea to remember which pins are left standing. I always say the numbers to myself just before I clear the pins. Then, just step on the treadle and reset the pin. And don't forget to release the treadle."

"That's it?" Vinnie said. "Hope I can remember the numbers. Sounds tough, eh, G?"

"Let's hear how you feel at the end of the day, wise guy," Borneo responded. "We turn on the open sign in fifteen minutes. Open bowling until two. Then the Monday women's summer league until four. Open bowling again until seven. Then the Monday beer league until closing. C'mon. Help me finish putting the oil mops away. Then you can practice setting pins."

CHAPTER 6

The first bowlers didn't come in until almost 12:20. "Hey Danny," Borneo said, "what time is it?"

Danny looked at his Timex and said, "You have to wait until the big hand is on the four. Then it will be twenty after twelve."

Borneo was clearly in charge of the cave. Yakky may have thought he was making decisions, but I doubted anything happened that wasn't approved by Borneo.

"What lanes are we on?" I asked.

Borneo replied, "I'll tell you when I see who's bowling out there. Just remember this, kid. You got no seniority, so you'll only be working when all six lanes are full or when someone needs a break or when you're told to take care of a lane. If you think life ain't fair in the cave, good, 'cause it ain't. Now get ready to set some pins."

Borneo winked at me. As rough as he looked, I had the sense that he would be fair about running the cave.

"You might want to take those shirts off, boys," Borneo said. "It's hot out there, and it gets even hotter in here." Borneo quickly removed his and threw it up on the seating planks. Danny did the same, but Albert and Crackers kept theirs on. Vinnie looked at me, we both shrugged our shoulders and removed our shirts. We couldn't help staring at Borneo. We had guessed him to be in his mid-twenties. Fully clothed, he was an imposing sight. He had twelve inches of thick, shiny black hair that extended almost perpendicular from his head in loose ringlets. On his slightly pockmarked face were bushy muttonchop sideburns and a well-formed mustache that dropped straight down from the sides of his mouth, ending in two sharp lines at the chin. It underlined a thick nose with large, round nostrils. His stomach distended slightly, although it did not seem the slightest bit flabby. His eyes were as black as his hair and had the appearance of bottomlessness. The removal of his shirt revealed a very large tattoo with the reddish green letters "1st Air Cav—Kim Son." covering his nearly hairless chest. He had a long, thin scar that ran most of the length from his armpit to his hip and a smaller, star-shaped scar just above his right nipple. He appeared well enough muscled to press Volkswagens. The longer one looked at him, the easier it was to speculate where he might have gotten his name.

At the head of the lane, a man and a woman, both with white hair, were tightening the laces on the red, tan, and green bowling shoes. Borneo peered through the opening at the end of the lane. He said, "It's the Van Dykes. Nice old couple, but they still think it's 1932 and a quarter buys you the Blue Plate Special at Brownie's Diner." He grinned at me and Vinnie. "Okay, boys, looks like you're up."

In 1968, not many people owned bowling balls. Frank kept two full racks of dull black community balls next to the counter. As we would find out, most of them had nicks and even some nasty gouges, but rarely did customers complain. The Van Dykes methodically examined most of the balls and settled on two. Borneo barked at me, "Lane 3, G-man." He looked at Vinnie and told him to set the pins on lane four. Borneo said to Danny, "Better get the light pins or those two won't knock any down."

Danny handed me a cardboard box with ten wooden pins. I looked at Borneo, and he just nodded at me. I stepped on the treadle, locked it, grabbed two pins with each hand, just like Borneo had done, and started setting them. "Gotta pick it up a little bit," Borneo said. I set all ten, released the treadle, and jumped back to the planks. Nothing happened, and then I heard, "Four pin."

I looked at Borneo, and he was stifling a laugh. A little louder this time. "Four pin!" I shrugged my shoulders and held my palms up. Borneo was hardly able to contain himself. "You have to reset the four pin, kid" Borneo said.

"Why?" I asked.

"Because the old man thinks it isn't setting on the right spot."

I protested slightly. "But I put it right on the peg."

"Look kid," Borneo said, "he says the four pin is off, humor him. Reach over gently and make it look like you are resetting the pin. Trust me. It'll work just fine."

I reached over, jiggled the pin slightly and withdrew.

I heard, "Ready to bowl," from the top of the lane, and then the sound of the bowling ball pounding against the oiled wood. In a few seconds, the ball crashed into the pins and sent most of them flying into the pit. The sound was deafening. Borneo, Danny, and Crackers were all busy putting cotton in their ears. "Oh yeah," Borneo yelled, "Don't forget to bring some cotton to work."

I jumped down from the planks and into the pit. One of the pins was still slightly spinning when I grabbed it. Borneo immediately said, "What are you doing? If a pin is moving, no matter how little, you never touch it. *Never.* That's one of the reasons some of the best bowlers prefer pin boys. Those automatic machines grab pins that are wobbling and clear some that are still rolling. You touch the wrong pin at the wrong time, you'll have more trouble than you'll ever need."

The Van Dykes finished three games each, none of which were exceptional. They only complained about the pin spotting three more times, which didn't seem so bad. I was a little slow at first, but by the third game, I was feeling more confident. There was a rhythm to pin setting. The trick was to not think about it but just let your hands move. It was hard work. It was hot and noisy and dirty in the cave. But it was…gratifying.

By then, all the other lanes were filled with bowlers, and all the pin boys were hard at work. "I think they're done," I yelled to Borneo. He tossed me and Vinnie each a tennis ball, and when I caught mine I could feel it had a small slit cut into it.

"Roll the tennis ball down to them," Borneo said. "They'll know what to do."

We rolled the balls down the return and in a minute they came bouncing back down the alley. Vinnie and I squeezed them and reached inside.

We held up the contents of the tennis ball. We looked at each other and simultaneously said, "A dime?"

Borneo laughed. "You guys must have done great work. Put those dimes in your pocket and remember what it feels like to get your first tip. See that chalk sitting on the plank? Write your name on the back wall and mark the number of games down. That way you make sure Yakky doesn't cheat you."

Business was fairly steady all day, and by 10:00 p.m. I had set pins for twenty-five lines and accumulated almost ten dollars in tips, two of which came from a happy guy who had the high game of 240 in the evening beer league. I learned everybody in the league put a dollar in a pot at the beginning of the night, and high game got to keep the whole thing, about fifty dollars that night.

"Nice goin', G," Borneo said. "First night on the job and you already got a high game tip. Just don't expect to get lucky every night."

Vinnie and I grabbed our shirts off the planks. We were tired, sore, and filthy, and our ears were ringing with the sounds of a thousand thunderous collisions of hard rubber and wood against each other.

"You think we should have called home?" I asked Vinnie.

"I didn't even think of it," he replied. "You gonna be in trouble?"

"If I don't show up tomorrow, go to Kelley's. I'll be the small casket in the back."

"C'mon, let's go get our money from Yakky," Vinnie said.

We collected our money and turned to leave.

"Hey, pin boys." It was Frank still apparently studying the *Daily News*. "We start at ten tomorrow. Be on time."

"We'll be here," Vinnie said. He looked at me with a grin. "Did you hear that, G? He called us pin boys."

CHAPTER 7

It didn't go as badly with my parents as I thought. My mother thought for sure I had been kidnaped by gypsies, even though gypsies hadn't ever been spotted in that part of New York State or the United States for that matter. My father seemed most irritated that he was not able to go to sleep at his customary nine, thereby causing him to watch a show called Family Affair, which he thought was possibly the dumbest show anyone had ever put on TV.

Just before I walked in, he said, "Hey, Tessie, what kind of-a parents name their boy Jody? That's a girl name. And then they name-a their girl Bumpy?"

"That's Buffy," she said. "And what are you worried about a stupid TV show when your son is not home when he's supposed to be."

"Have you ever seen this piece of-a crap?" he asked. "It's a old guy and a fat guy with a funny accent who live in this apartment with these kids who never make-a no mess. You ever seen kids who never make-a no mess?"

"*Mannaggia*, Tommy Petrosino. You need to do something. What if he was kidnaped by gypsies?"

"Ah, don't worry," Tommy said. "Him and that *gabagool* Antonioni are too lucky to get into any real trouble." But the look on his face said he wasn't sure if he believed that.

It was a short walk from the bowling alley to our house. Both my parents were outside on the front stoop when I walked up at 10:20 p.m. They both turned, and I followed them inside. My mother started in on me right away and didn't let me say much other than, "Yes, Ma, you're right, Ma, it won't happen again, Ma." She was just getting into a rhythm when my little brother Anthony started wailing.

"Now look what you've done. You woke up your brother. Now I'll be up all night trying to get him back to sleep. I hope you're happy."

I didn't think it would be a good idea to remind her I hadn't actually been the one yelling. Then it was my father's turn.

"Where you been?" he asked.

"I got a job today. At the Riverbend Alleys. I'm a pin boy."

My father had never bowled in his life, unless you counted bocce ball. "What kind of-a job is pin boy? And how did you get so filthy?"

I explained it to him, and when I was finished, he cuffed me lightly on the back of the head and said, "Next time, call your mother. Take a bath and go to bed."

I set my alarm for nine and didn't wake up until the irritating buzz filled the room. I rolled out of bed feeling like someone must have come into my room during the night and tenderized me with a wooden bat. I washed and went down to the kitchen where my mother had just started a pot of oatmeal. There was a knock on the back door, and when I looked through the curtain, I saw Vinnie.

"Good morning, Mrs. Petrosino," he said as I let him in.

"*Buon giorno*, Vincenz'," she replied.

"I see you're making oatmeal," he said. "I've always told G you make the best oatmeal in the neighborhood. You must have a secret recipe or something."

She smiled slightly. Even though she could easily see through Vinnie, his charm was still irresistible. "Don't worry, there's plenty enough for two hardworking pin boys here."

I toasted some white bread, covered it with butter and grape jelly, offered Vinnie a piece, and ate it while the oatmeal was simmering. During breakfast, my mother made baloney sandwiches on white bread with mustard and put them in a brown bag along with some dried figs and walnuts. My mother thought dried figs and walnuts were nature's equivalent of super mega vitamins. I thought they might at least kill the taste of the baloney on white.

We made it to the bowling alley at 9:55 a.m. Frank was in his office reading the paper and smoking a Lucky. Yakky was powdering shoes. Borneo was sitting on a bench, staring at nothing in particular. Danny was showing Albert his watch again. The door opened behind us and in walked a girl.

"We're not open until noon," I said. "You have to come back then."

She looked directly at Vinnie and me. "I work here. Who are you two bozos?"

Vinnie jumped in first. "Allow me to introduce ourselves. We're the new pin boys. I'm Vinnie Antonioni. This is my faithful sidekick, G, also known as Gianni Petrosino. I'm sure you've probably heard of us."

"Actually, no," she said. Her tone softened slightly. "I've only been in Riverbend a little over two weeks. My father is the new pastor for the First Presbyterian Church. But I'm sure you'll be telling me all about yourselves. And I can hardly wait to hear it. Some other time."

Before she could walk away, Vinnie said, "Hey, don't tell me you're—"

"I'm Sally Gibb," she said. "But in the cave, you can call me Charlie Horse." Then she turned to me and said, "Does he do all your talking?" She held my eye for the briefest of moments, turned, and walked away.

Vinnie looked at me and said, "She's not Italian, she's not Catholic, and she's a girl."

"She sure is," I said. "She's definitely a girl." For a moment, I felt a little lightheaded, but I figured it had to be that overpowering smell of bananas. I mean, what else could it have been?

CHAPTER 8

Danny looked at his Timex and announced, "It's ten o'clock now. Ten o'clock."

Borneo and Albert went to a closet near Frank's office and retrieved two mops and two medium-sized metal containers that were clearly marked Banana Oil. At least that explained the smell of bananas. It also explained why I had no desire to eat a banana for years afterward.

Borneo said, "All right, Charlie Horse, you got garbage and cleanup out front. Danny, you help her."

Danny looked devastated. "But I always do the lane oil, Borneo."

"I know," Borneo said, "but we gotta teach the new guys how it's done in case they have to do it on your day off. You'll be back on it tomorrow."

"Okay, Borneo," he said, and just like that, his grin returned.

Borneo continued, "Albert, you oil up one, two, and three. Antonioni, you got cleanup in the cave. There's a broom in the closet. Sweep it out best you can. G-man, you learn how to oil a lane this morning. Your turn tonight, Antonioni."

Yakky emerged from behind the counter and walked over to where Borneo, Vinnie, and I were standing. Borneo seemed unhappy Yakky didn't stick to powdering shoes.

"Lemme tell you a few things you don't know about bowling lanes," Yakky started. "Well, first, sometimes they refer to bowling as kegling, and they call the bowlers keglers. It's a German word that means bowling. Bet you've seen that 'cause they use that in the newspaper all the time. Now, any lane that's built these days has real specific measurements. Back in the old days, a lot of lanes were built almost by eyeball. Turns out, this alley was built a little less than a year after the first American Bowling Congress meeting in New York City, so the people who built these lanes might have had some specifications, but none of us really knows for sure. Even so, it turns out Riverbend Alleys is within the official specifications, so any records set here count. All the lanes are forty-two inches wide, and it's sixty feet from the foul line to where the head pin sits. See how the wood changes color a little way down the lane? All this approach area and the first sixteen feet of the lane are made from rock maple. It's a really hard wood, so even if you drop a ball on it, it don't leave any dents. And believe me, some guys throw the ball down the lane quite a way before it drops. They used the same maple wood back on the pin deck, which is the last four feet of the lane. In between the lane is some kind of pine. Pine's a good wood if you want some friction on the ball to make it curve." Yakky was happy to have the chance to impress someone with his knowledge.

Borneo had heard it all before. "Think I can show them how to oil those maple and pine lanes now?" he said. His irritation at being put off was barely noticeable. Vinnie grabbed a broom and headed down to the cave.

There were specially designed lane mops for applying the banana oil to the wood.

"I don't know for sure why they use banana oil," Borneo said, "but I'm sure Yakky knows."

Borneo explained that only the first thirty-five feet or so of the lane was oiled. "There's a mark on the side of the lane to tell you where the oil stops. The ball slides on the oil and doesn't spin as much. When it hits the dry part of the lane, the ball really grabs hold and gets that hook the good bowlers put on it. We usually try to get the oil pretty even, but the center is usually a little slicker than the edges 'cause that's where we spray the oil." He showed me how to spray the oil from the can, how to work it with the lane mop, and how to buff it so it looked shiny and even. It wasn't a hard job, but Borneo warned me that the really good bowlers could tell when a lane wasn't oiled properly.

"Now the fun part," Borneo said. "Grab a ball."

I went over to the racks, found one that felt pretty good, and went back to the lane. "Okay, G-man," Borneo said, "roll it down the lane just like you were bowling. We're gonna test out that oil job."

At that point, it occurred to me that I had never actually launched a bowling bowl down a lane before. I looked at the ball. There were three holes, one of which was obviously for the thumb.

Borneo said, "The middle finger and the fourth finger."

I did my best to imitate the bowlers I had seen the day before, striding up to the line and letting the ball go. It made it about halfway down the lane before it dropped off into the gutter.

"Well, that didn't tell us much, did it," Borneo said. "Watch me." He yelled at Vinnie, "Hey, Antonioni. Roll that ball back."

Borneo stepped up to the lane and spun the ball at where the pins would have been. It looked to me like he would have caught the head pin dead center.

"Why don't you buff that out just a bit more," he said. "Seems just a hair too slick."

With Borneo's help, I finished the last two lanes. Riverbend Alleys looked about as clean as we were going to get it. We put all the cleaning things away and filed down the lane to the cave.

CHAPTER 9

Tuesday afternoon was not very busy. Outside, it was warm and sunny. Inside the bowling alley, it was just warm. By three o'clock, I had only managed to pick up two games and a quarter in tips.

Borneo said, "On nice days like this, people have better things to do than hang out at an unrefrigerated bowling alley." He poured water from a pitcher into a hard plastic cup and took a long drink. "Frank don't do much for us, but we get all the water we want back here."

I grabbed my lunch bag and nibbled my way through the baloney sandwich. I plucked the plastic-wrapped parcel of dried figs and walnuts out of the bag and opened it. I used the tried and true method of taking one fig, placing a walnut on top of it, and popping it all into my mouth.

Danny asked, "What are those things?"

"These?" I replied. "They're dried figs and walnuts."

"What's a fig?"

"I dunno. A fruit I guess. It comes from a tree."

Danny seemed satisfied with that. "I like corn on the cob," he said. "With lots of butter and salt."

Things picked up a little bit in the late afternoon, although we never had a time when all the lanes were busy at once.

"Don't worry," Borneo said, "tonight you get to work your rear end off."

At around six, Borneo went up front, checked the oil on the alleys, and decided to lightly dress them all. When he came back to the cave, he said, "Let's go, Antonioni. Time to get you trained on lane oiling." Borneo looked around the cave. "Where's Albert?"

Vinnie said, "I saw him bolt out the front door about fifteen minutes ago. Maybe he went to get some dinner."

"Right," Borneo said. He sounded more concerned than peeved. "Okay, Danny, you're back oiling. Take four, five, and six. G and Charlie Horse, you two take a break."

I looked at her, trying to think of something clever to say. All I came up with was, "Want a root beer?"

"No," she said, "but I'll have a grape."

We bought our sodas from Yakky—Frank's rules were no free sodas—and sat on one of the benches. After a minute or two of silence, I said, "So do you like Riverbend?"

"I don't know," she said. "It doesn't feel right to me, but I guess that's because it's different."

"Where are you from?"

"New Jersey. Close to Philadelphia."

"What was it like there that was so different?"

"I don't know," she said. "It doesn't look a whole lot different. Lots of trees and water, just like here. My mom used to take me to Philadelphia to see all the Christmas decorations and shop at the big department stores. There aren't any big cities with lots of lights or tall buildings near Riverbend. That's different. I guess it just felt like home. I suppose I have to give Riverbend a chance to feel like home too."

"I know what you mean," I said. "Three times a year, my parents pack us up to spend the holidays with my relatives in Brooklyn. Whenever I come out of the Lincoln Tunnel into Manhattan, I don't know—it just feels like I belong there. I like the lights and all the people and the big buildings."

"I've never been to New York City," she said, "much less Brooklyn."

"Why'd you leave New Jersey?" I asked.

"You sure ask a lot of questions for a boy who lets his friend do all his talking." She stared straight ahead, almost as if she was looking for someone. Then, she looked down at the floor, her voice dropping nearly to a whisper. "It was a great opportunity for my dad," she said. "Let's go see how your friend Vinnie is doing." She grabbed her grape soda and walked over to where Vinnie and Borneo were buffing the lanes.

I couldn't figure out why she left so quickly. I thought we were getting along just fine. I noticed I felt a little lightheaded again. That banana oil was powerful stuff.

CHAPTER 10

"Hey, Borneo," I yelled, "I'm goin' outside for a last breath of fresh air. That okay?"

"Yeah," he replied. "But don't wander away. We got some work to do to get ready for the Pro League at seven. We're all gonna be busy tonight."

I went out the front door and walked around back toward the river. Albert was there, sitting on the ground with his back against the building and his legs stretched out in front of him. In his left hand was a paper bag that held a bottle of some kind. He moved it to his mouth and took a long swig.

"Hey, Albert. Borneo was wondering where you were."

Albert stood up and brushed some of the dirt from his pants. He looked at me with his odd smile. "It was hot in there, G. I needed something to cool me down." Then he took another swig.

I said, "Borneo says we need everyone tonight. It's gonna be busy."

"I know. It's Pro League. I might sneak away for a little bit in the afternoon, but I'm always there for Pro League. You go inside and tell Borneo I'll be right there."

I hesitated a moment.

Albert said, "I'll be fine, little G. I just need to cool off a little." He spit out a throaty laugh. "I might even take a little swim in the river. I'll see you in the cave."

Even though I had the sense that Albert was bothered by something, I didn't have a better response than to head back inside the bowling alley. I looked back once more at Albert. He was sitting down again, his chin resting on his collarbone, both arms wrapped around the paper bag with the bottle in it. He must have sensed me looking because he turned his head in my direction, smiled his crooked smile, and went back to draining the bottle's contents.

I told Borneo Albert was outside in the back of the building. "Good," he said. "Don't want to be pulling any extra doubles tonight."

"Borneo," I said, "what's bothering Albert? He seems like such a nice man, but outside, he looked like the unhappiest person I ever saw."

"I try not to get too involved in other people's problems, G-man. I got enough of my own to worry about. Round up everyone and meet me up front. I'll go get Albert."

I was pretty sure I wasn't going to avoid getting involved. As Vinnie would note years later when I pushed my way on to the student council, I couldn't stand still when something—or someone—bothered me.

By the time Borneo got back with Albert, Yakky was already on a roll.

"We got three kinds of pins here at bowling alley," Yakky said, directing it mostly at me and Vinnie. "The biggest pins are called the kingpins. Know why we call 'em the kingpins?" Vinnie and I had no clue, but we were certain Yakky would tell us. He didn't pause long enough to get an answer. "Just look at 'em. They got this painted thing that looks like a crown around the neck of the pin. All done by hand too. I don't know if that's where the term kingpin comes from, but I tell everybody it is. They're the kings of the pins. They're made of hardwood, but they can still get chipped or even cracked. We actually got a guy who fixes 'em up and paints 'em when they need it. I weighed one once. Three and a half pounds, more or less. You gotta hit those pins with a lot of force to make them go down, so only the best bowlers use them. The recreational bowlers use what we call the light pins. They don't weigh a lot less, but they're just enough so women and weaker bowlers can get them to fly around. Pin boys hate the light pins, ain't that right, Danny?"

Danny nodded his head, mostly out of expectation. Danny had a tendency to agree with pretty much everyone.

"The third type of pin...actually, you'll find out about that later. Just remember, tonight it's all kingpins. These guys comin' in are the best. Not just in Riverbend, but for quite a ways around. Ever see that show on Sunday mornings with the local bowlers? Lot of those guys bowl in the Pro League right here."

Borneo interrupted. "We need to get set up in the back, Yakky. I'm gonna check the lane oil, and then we'll get the pins set."

"Yeah, fine," Yakky said. "Charlie Horse, how 'bout you be foul line spotter for the early group tonight."

Borneo didn't put up an argument, so I assumed that would have been his choice as well.

"Bowlers got until 7:15 to warm up," Yakky said. "Just set those pins as fast as you can. Each team has five bowlers. After they're warmed up, each team bowls a three-game set. They supply their own scorekeepers and turn the sheets in to me at the end of the night. I take care of all the statistics and figuring handicaps and the like. They bowl quick, and they bowl serious.

"Danny, you can have the double tonight."

Borneo once again didn't dispute Yakky's choice.

"Oh, one other thing," Yakky said. "Frank's had a standing prize of $1,000 for any team that rolls a combined score of 4,000 in a real league match. Ain't never been done, although the Big Belinos came pretty close once."

Vinnie said, "Big Belinos? Are you kidding?"

"What's a big belino?" Charlie Horse asked.

We all started laughing hard. "I can see you got a bit to learn about Italians," Vinnie said.

"Let's go, pin boys," Yakky said. "Let's go to work."

CHAPTER 11

By seven o'clock, the place was full of serious bowlers. Every one of them had his own shoes and a bowling ball that he carried in a slick leather bag. They were dressed in bright, colorful shirts that hung loosely outside their neatly pressed pants. Team names like Lucky Strikes, Rolling Thunder, Ten Pin Alley, Spare Parts, Lickety Splits, and of course, Big Belinos were embroidered across the shirt back, while the names and nicknames of each bowler were threaded above the front pocket.

Bowlers were rolling practice balls one right after the other and everyone but Albert seemed to be struggling to keep pace. All of a sudden, the balls stopped rolling. Vinnie looked at me, and I looked at Borneo. Borneo peered past the pin deck, then turned to us and said, "It's Mingo."

Both Vinnie and I intoned at the same time, "Mingo? What's a Mingo?"

"Mingo," Borneo said, "is the best bowler in Riverbend. Maybe the best bowler in New York state, 'cept for Peckham."

There was a simultaneous shout of "Mingo" from the front of the lane, and then the bowlers went back to warming up.

"Looks like Danny gets Mingo and the Belinos tonight," Borneo said. He looked at me and Vinnie. "Consider yourselves lucky."

Danny exclaimed, "It's quarter after seven. It's time for the bowlers to start."

Vinnie and I worked our best to keep up, but it was difficult. There were lots of strikes, and the bowlers barely paused between rolls. Even with cotton in our ears, it was noisy, and the air in the cave was stale and stifling. It didn't help that most of the bowlers constantly puffed on cigarettes and cigars, especially the acrid DiNobilis. By

THE KINGPINS OF RIVERBEND

nine o'clock, Vinnie and I were wondering if we would last until the league finished. Even Borneo and Albert looked like they were struggling a bit.

Borneo was the first to pick up on the growing buzz at the head of Danny's lanes. "Something is happening up there," he said. "You can feel it. Hey, Danny, what's going on?"

"I don't know, Borneo. But I think the Belinos have been doing pretty good tonight. I can tell there's been a lot of strikes."

"I wonder if..." Borneo started. The other lanes seemed to be slowing down and bowlers were drifting over to where the Belinos were rolling. Borneo peeked through the pin deck and looked at where Charlie Horse was calling the foul line violations. She mouthed, "Four thousand."

Borneo was excited. "Hey, boys, the Belinos have a chance at four thousand. Okay, Danny. Set 'em up good." He looked back out at Charlie Horse.

"Eighth frame," she mouthed.

"Three more frames," Borneo said to us.

In the eighth frame, all the Belinos rolled strikes and did it again in the ninth. All the other lanes had stopped, and everyone was gathered behind the Belinos. All the pin boys, except for Danny, left the cave to watch the last frame. Even Frank stopped reading the *Daily News* and walked out to watch the tenth frame. Five bowlers would each bowl their tenth frame. Fifteen strikes would give them exactly four thousand pins and the thousand dollars to split. Frank's pallor looked a little more ashen. Danny set the pins on lane four. It was dead quiet when the Belino bowler sent a perfect ball into the one-three pocket. The pins collided with each other and none were left standing. The place erupted with an enormous roar. Danny reset the pins, another perfect roll, and another strike. The cheer this time seemed even louder. It was the same result on the third ball. Four bowlers to go.

It was three more strikes from the next Belino bowler and another three strikes from the next. Two bowlers to go. The penultimate Belino bowler rolled two solid strikes. The third ball hit slightly high. Nine pins went down, but the ten pin wobbled, seemingly taking a half minute before it finally plopped over. One bowler and three strikes to go.

Danny set the pins, and Mingo stepped up to the lane. Even the men from the other teams were shouting encouragement.

"C'mon, Mingo."

"You can do it, Mingo."

"Show 'em how it's done, Mingo."

Mingo stepped up, looking as confident as the best bowler in town could look. There wasn't a whisper anywhere inside Riverbend Alleys as he approached the lane. As soon as he let the ball go, three dozen men and pin boys started yelling. His hook was perfect, and all tenpins scattered into the pit behind the pin deck. The roar was immense. Danny rolled the ball back to Mingo, reset the pins, and waited for the next roll.

Mingo cradled the ball, took five steps to the lane, and let another perfect hook go. The ball tracked perfectly to the pocket and once again the pins all toppled.

Mingo looked perfectly composed as he picked up the ball from the return. Danny finished setting the pins and hopped up to the plank. Mingo took his spot at the head of the lane, held the ball in his left hand, carefully placed his thumb and two middle fingers into the ball, and peered at the pins. He moved smoothly forward and let the ball fly. Everyone in the bowling alley screamed as the ball slid toward the pins. Mingo stayed in his finishing pose, waiting for the inevitable.

It was a solid tenpin. When all the pins had stopped spinning and rolling, the ten pin was still upright. A collective groan filtered through the group. His teammates slapped him on the back and said, "Great try, Mingo." Frank impassively went back to his office. The rest of us started back to the cave to finish the evening.

Mingo stared at the lone tenpin. Danny's head appeared as he started to clear the pins. Without warning, Mingo screamed at Danny, "You retard. You didn't set the tenpin right. I threw a perfect ball, and the ten pin didn't move because you're too retarded to set a pin right." Danny froze as Mingo grabbed a ball from the return and sent it flying down the lane. It hit the tenpin solidly, knocking it

off the sideboard and directly at Danny's face. He instinctively threw up his left hand to protect himself. The sideboard absorbed some of the force of the pin, but it was still moving hard enough to smash the face of Danny's Timex. Danny was unhurt, but the watch was destroyed.

Danny lifted his head, looked down the alley at Mingo, and then stared at his mangled watch. He shook it a few times as if that would magically make the hands start moving again. His face was contorted in an awful way, an awful and ugly way. He slid all the way through the opening, got to his feet and headed down the alley at Mingo.

Mingo yelled, "What are you doing, you retard? Why don't you slide back down that alley, go in your cave, and be a retard. You're a good for nothing imbecile."

Danny continued to advance up the lane, and when he was almost at the foul line, he stopped. "You broke my watch. You owe me a new watch. Give me a watch."

"I don't owe you anything retard," Mingo said. "You owe the Belinos a thousand dollars because you can't set a pin right."

Danny advanced on Mingo and the other Belinos moved to intercept him.

"Hey, Danny." It was Borneo moving from the right to insert himself between Danny and Mingo. "I need some help back in the cave. Come back with me."

"He owes me a watch," Danny said, "and I'm not going anywhere until I get it." Danny's bottom lip slid up over his top lip, and there was no hint of his usual smile.

"Why don't you let me talk to him. Go back and help Vinnie and G."

Danny looked at Borneo.

"It's okay, Danny," Borneo said quietly. "I'll take care of it. I'll take care of getting you a watch."

Danny's hands balled into fists, but just as suddenly, he let them relax and slowly headed back down the alley to the cave. Borneo turned to Mingo and the other Belinos. In a low, controlled voice, he said, "If you ever hurt another one of the pin boys, you'll deal with me. And believe me. You wouldn't want to deal with me. And one other thing. Without Danny's watch, we can't tell time back in the cave. So you and the other Belinos think about how you are going to make sure we can tell time. 'Cause if we can't tell time, we can't tell when we're supposed to set pins for you guys. It was a Timex. A real good Timex."

"You don't scare me you…wild man," Mingo said. "You're not much better than that retard you're protecting."

Borneo glared at Mingo. "You might ask the rest of the Belinos how quick they'll be to step in front of me when I explain it to you face to fist. I mean face. Face to face. Tomorrow is Danny's day off. I'll bet he'd just love to have a nice new Timex delivered to his house. Think about it, Mingo. And stop letting your mouth get the rest of you in trouble."

Borneo went back to the cave and found Danny sitting on the plank staring at his watch. "It isn't moving, Borneo."

"Don't worry, Danny. The Belinos will take care of getting you a new Timex. Come on. Let's finish off the night. It was pretty exciting, huh? Frank almost had to pay those Belinos a grand. Let's get finished and go home."

CHAPTER 12

Mayor David Greene sat behind his enormous wood desk and wondered how he could have ever agreed to run for office. He rubbed a hand through his thinning black hair three times, let out a large sigh, picked up his telephone, and dialed a familiar number. After five rings, a sleepy voice grunted an unfriendly hello at him.

"And a pleasant good morning to you too," Greene said.

The man on the other end of the line was Tony Gallo, kingmaker in a town where being king was mostly a royal pain in the ass. He had held the official title of Director of Public Works for the last thirty years and figured as long as his body held out, he might just do another thirty years. He was a large man, standing six foot three and weighing a full three hundred fifty pounds. He had an enormous head that was still full of curly black hair and a wide gap between his two front teeth that accentuated his already toothy smile.

Of course, it was well-known that he wouldn't drop dead from overwork, showing up at his office at the city yard not more than once every two weeks to sign a contract or approve an invoice, most of which were to companies in which he was the majority, albeit very silent, partner. As he shook some of the sleep from his head, he wondered how drunk he must have been to think putting that Jewish outsider Greene in the mayor's office was a good idea.

"Davey," said Gallo in his graveled voice, "you're up and at 'em early today."

"It's ten o'clock, Tony. City government's been serving the people for a couple of hours now."

"Yeah, well some of us are so efficient we can finish eight hours of work in an hour." Tony started thinking that in all the time he and his cronies had been taking care of business, there had never been a more irritating, ungrateful, clueless bastard than Greene. There were actually days the sonofabitch thought he was in charge. Just last month when Tony told him Public Works needed some extra cash this year because the locker room at the golf course needed some improvements, like cherry lockers and a whirlpool tub, the big shot mayor told him he didn't know and "would have to take it under consideration." Tony almost told him he might also consider how his size eleven Italian foot might feel up his ass, but instead said, "Thanks, Davey. I'm sure you'll take care of things." Then he mentally calculated how many more days it was until the next election.

"You up for lunch today, Tony?" The way Greene said it, it sounded like a slam at Tony's 350-pound frame. "My treat."

Tony thought if that cheap *stronzo* was buying lunch, he finally figured out how much serious trouble he had.

"Of course, Davey. How's twelve thirty at Isabella's? Not too spicy for you, is it?"

"Isabella's is fine," Greene said. "I haven't had their chicken parm in a while."

Chicken parm, thought Tony. Italian food for people who don't know the difference. "I'll see you there," Tony said, and hung up the phone. He rolled himself up and sat on the edge of the bed. *What did I do to deserve this?* he wondered.

"Hey, Tony," his wife yelled from downstairs, "you want some breakfast?"

The voice went through him like an icy wind blowing across the river. He lifted his eyes skyward and momentarily thought about how wonderful it would be to catch his wife and David Greene together in bed. Then he could take care of two headaches at once. Too bad his wife had a face and body that would make death row inmates look forward to the chair.

"Thanks, honey," he said. "Some sausage and peppers and eggs with Italian bread would be nice. I'm going to shower. I'll be down in twenty minutes."

She idly wondered whether or not sausage would cover the taste of rat poison. "Okay, sweetheart. I'll get it started."

David Greene was already sitting at a table reading a menu when Tony Gallo arrived at ten to one. Before arriving, Tony was across the street watching for Greene to show up. He thought, "I'll be damned if I'm going to wait for that asshole." After Greene went inside, he waited another ten minutes, just to make sure Greene got the message of who was in charge here.

"Tony," Greene said, "glad you could make it. Want a drink? Some scotch? A little chianti?"

Paying for drinks too, Tony thought, *he must really think he's in the soup.* "It's a bit early for me, Davey. I think I'll just have some Vichy water."

He signaled the waiter over and ordered the sparkling water, no ice.

"So this is a pleasure I don't often get," Tony said. "What's the occasion? You're not resigning on me, are you?" Of course not, Tony thought. The little weasel was too dumb to know he was in over his head. The waiter returned with the drink and placed it on a square white napkin. Tony took a small sip.

"I'll get right to it," Greene said. "The city is pretty much in the fiscal toilet. Half the factories are empty, and nobody is paying any taxes on those places. People are leaving town like we been hit by the plague, and a lot of them aren't even bothering to sell their houses, mostly because they wouldn't be worth enough to make them give a crap. Property tax collections are down a third. The water system has more leaky pipes than ones that work, and the state is telling me maybe there'll be some grant money next year, but don't count on it. The high school building needs more repairs than I could list. I'd have to float a bond just to buy some new office furniture."

"What's wrong with the furniture you got, Davey?"

"Come on, Tony, get serious. How you gonna feel when your garbage men miss a paycheck?"

"Look, we both know that ain't gonna happen." Tony put on his best, I'll-take-care-of-everything face.

"Tony, I'm not going down as the mayor who bankrupted the city. When things hit the fan, I'm not the only one likely to get splattered."

Tony's purplish face belied his calmer demeanor. He held up a fork and looked directly at Greene. "Davey," he said, "two things. One, you don't panic until I tell you it's time to panic, and it ain't time to panic, *capisce*? And two, and this is real important for you to listen to, you think long and hard about what a bad idea it would be for you to not be a standup guy. The buck stops right at your office. You think it's ever gonna look any other way, then maybe you ain't been paying attention for the last thirty years. You ain't the mayor 'cause of your incredible skills as a politician. Don't forget that."

Greene put his hands in the air in a mock gesture of surrender. "Geez, Tony," he said, "don't misunderstand me. You can count on me no matter what." He leaned over the table. "Really. I'm a rock."

"C'mon, Davey," Tony said. "I know I can depend on you." The waiter brought their lunches, chicken parmesan for Greene, and linguine with white clam sauce for Tony. "Hey, the food looks delicious. Let's eat and then you can tell me your ideas for getting things fixed. That's what I'm best at, Davey. Fixing things." He raised his glass of Vichy water, cracked a toothy smile, and said, "*Salud.*"

Greene replied, "*Mazeltov.*"

The rest of lunch was mostly small talk, how's the wife and kids, summer's been a little too damn hot, the Yankees got beat again the other night. Tony ordered an espresso and a cannoli for dessert, Greene just a regular coffee.

Tony started the conversation. "You know, Davey, in thirty years as head of the public works, I learned two important things. First, things are never as bad as they seem right when they happen. Second, always trust in the Lord, and in this town, I am the Lord." He chuckled at his own cleverness.

"Tony, if you got a plan, I'm all ears."

"Davey, the plan is simple. What do you do when you're the most miserable? When everything's the darkest?"

"You're asking a Jew what he does when he is most miserable? You gotta be kidding. That would be between when we get up and when we go to bed."

"Well, I can tell you what the Italians do. We have a party. A big celebration. Nothing makes you forget about what's bothering you quicker than a feast."

Greene tilted his head to the side and scrunched his forehead. "What are you saying? We need to have a party? That's the answer to watching the whole place circling the bowl?"

Tony shook his head. "Don't you get it? It ain't the party. It's the anticipation. The distraction. As long as people got something to occupy their minds, they won't worry about their troubles. We need to give them something to look forward to. Something that'll keep them busy and out of our hair while we solve the other problem. Then, once the party's over, we'll have things taken care of and nobody will know the difference. You think this is the first time we've had this kind of trouble? You think when the Wortham plant shut down things weren't twice as bad? They left five hundred people without a job, and five hundred more who depended on them for business, and five hundred more who depended on them, and so on. We got through that, and we'll get through this. We just need to distract everyone for a couple of months while we figure it out."

The mayor shifted in his chair. "Okay, Tony, we have a party. As long as it doesn't cost anything. In case I wasn't clear before, we can't afford a package of franks."

Tony was taking great delight in stringing Greene along. He knew the problem was coming before Greene did, and he already had most of the plan worked out. When his old friend Jacky Di Felipo called two days ago, it was like a gift from God. Riverbend would have a party all right. A party that would make them forget about all their troubles. A party that would make Riverbend a whole new town. The people would flock back to Riverbend, and Tony Gallo would be back on top again. Tony thought that genius like his should be bottled and sold like tonic. He had everything figured out.

Everything except Gianni Petrosino.

"Gimme a day or two, Davey," Tony said. "Meanwhile, call Jimmy at the bank. He'll keep us floating for a while. In a day or two, I'll have it all worked out. Trust me."

"I hope so, Tony. I really hope so."

CHAPTER 13

The first two weeks went by quickly. Vinnie proved to be almost as much a natural pinsetter as Danny. I struggled keeping up with everyone else the first week, but by the end of the second week, I was competent enough to stop being noticed. Borneo thought it might help if I stopped watching Charlie Horse set pins when I had a lane to take care of. Funny, I thought, I didn't even realize I was doing it. After all, I was thirteen years old and thought girls were gross.

Borneo thought Vinnie should have Wednesday off, which made my day off Thursday. I protested a little, since Thursday was one of the Pro League days, meaning the tips were always better. But Vinnie was a better pinsetter than I was, and I had to agree that it made more sense for him to work Thursday night.

My mother and Mrs. Antonioni started making a habit of showing up at the bowling alley around four thirty most days, bringing with them enough food to give everyone at least a taste. Borneo especially appreciated the home-cooked food.

"My," my mother would say, "you have a bigger appetite than all these other boys put together."

Borneo looked embarrassed and said, "I'm sorry, Mrs. Petrosino. It's just that this food is so good I can't help myself."

"Don't you apologize for anything," she said. "Anybody who likes my food can eat as much of it as they want. *Mangia*, Mr. Borneo."

Before they left, they usually dropped off something for Frank.

"It's not healthy to be that skinny, you know," Mrs. Antonioni said to Frank.

Frank looked up from the *Daily News*, shrugged his shoulders, and said, "Maybe if I keep eating your cooking I won't be so skinny."

One Wednesday, my mother brought a large pan of meat and sausage lasagna. By now, she knew everyone's name and said hello to each one as she saw them. "Hello, Mr. Frank, and you too, Mr. Yakky. How are you today, Mr. Danny? You going to have some lasagna, Mr. Albert?"

Albert smiled sheepishly and nodded his head.

"Why don't I leave it here, and you can bring the pan home with you tonight, Gianni," she said to me.

Yakky produced some paper plates and plastic utensils from behind the snack bar. He said, "Bring Frank the first piece. Then he won't complain about us using up the high class dinnerware."

Seldom was there anyone bowling around dinnertime, so we usually got to sit out front and eat our dinner. Charlie Horse and I sat together on one of the team benches.

"What exactly is lasagna, G?" she asked.

"It's these long, flat noodles filled with different cheeses, tomato sauce, and meat. It's my favorite meal."

She took a small bite and smiled. "It is good," she said. "My father doesn't make a lot of fancy stuff for us. Mostly meat and potatoes and canned vegetables. He never cooked much before we moved here. That was my mother's job. She made the best turkey and mashed potatoes you ever ate."

I noticed she had let her hair down. Usually, in the cave, she wore it pinned up at the top of her head or in a long braid. It was quite long, almost touching the small of her back, and had a color that was somewhere between brown and blonde.

"You like Riverbend any better?" I asked.

"It's hard to say," she answered. "The people seem nice enough. On Sunday when they shake hands with my father after the service, they all seem very kind to him. Some of the church ladies leave food for Sunday dinner. I guess they know how busy he is on Sunday. We have a long service on Sunday morning. My father works hard to write a good sermon, but lately, most of his sermons seem to be sad and talking about how God has lots of different plans for each of us and how even if we don't like the plan, we have to accept it. He used to read his sermons to my mother, and she would tell him how wonderful his words were and how they were sure to inspire the congregation. I told him he could read them to me, but he hasn't yet. On Sunday night, we have a Bible study group where we look at different parts of the Bible and talk about it. Last week, we talked about Job. It made me feel better because he had it a lot worse than I ever did. But Riverbend doesn't feel like home yet. It feels like someplace to be while we figure out where we are going."

"It must be hard," I said, "just you and your dad."

"It is," she said. She paused. "Let's talk about something else."

"How did you get to be called Charlie Horse?" I asked. "That's a pretty strange name for a girl."

She finally laughed. "Oh, that. Well, the first day I was here, my legs weren't used to all the bending, and they kept cramping on me. Every time I would get a cramp, one of the guys would yell, hey, it's another Charlie Horse. So that became my nickname. I wasn't like you, coming here with a nickname already. But if you want, when we aren't in the cave, I don't mind if you call me Sally."

"Okay, Sally. But you can still just call me G."

She looked contemplative. "I don't know. I sort of liked the way Gianni sounded when your mother said it. It sounds like singing when you say the name. How about I call you Gianni and you call me Sally when the others aren't around."

"I like that. Gianni and Sally."

We talked a little more about what things we liked and didn't like in school and what our favorite TV shows were. By the time everyone was done eating, there was only a small piece left in the pan. "Maybe you can take this home to your father," I said to Sally. "I bet he'll like it. We'll wrap it in something. Just don't forget."

A little after six, people started drifting into the bowling alley. Borneo asked Danny what time it was, and Danny held up his new Timex and said, "It's ten after six, Borneo. You like my new watch? It's a beauty."

"Hey, Danny," Borneo said, "without you and your watch, we would never know when it was time to set pins."

Things stayed pretty slow until around eight, and Borneo talked about maybe letting Sally and me go home early, but at eight, a group of three older teenage couples came in to bowl. The boys were what we called greasers, with big, slicked back hair, white T-shirts with cigarettes rolled up in the sleeve, tight-fitting blue jeans, white socks, and shiny black shoes. The girls wore pretty much the same outfit, but with loud red lipstick and matching painted nails.

Borneo said, "Don't worry. They're just here to have fun, just like everyone else. Charlie Horse, why don't you take one of the lanes. Albert and Crackers, you take the other two."

I started watching them as they changed into bowling shoes. The boys were loud and aggressive, pushing and shoving and playfully punching each other. The girls looked irritated with them and bored with the whole idea of bowling.

One of them yelled, "Hey, we need the light pins so the girls can knock them down." Borneo nodded to Danny. "Get the light pins. Set 'em up."

At first, they seemed to bowl with some seriousness, but after a few frames, it was clear none of them was very interested in a good score. The real trouble started in the seventh frame. One of the boys on Crackers' lane left five pins, and as Crackers went to clear the pins, he sent a second ball rolling toward him. Crackers heard the sound of the ball hitting the alley and barely cleared out of the way before it would have smashed into him. He yelled up the alley, "Hey, wait until I clear the pins before you roll another ball."

The greaser boys thought this was hilarious and started laughing at Crackers. They started using the lighter balls favored by the girls. This enabled them to throw much harder, sending the light pins flying across alleys. Borneo yelled at them to slow down and use the heavier balls, but this only seemed to spur them on. I looked at Borneo and said, "Why don't we do something? These guys are gonna hurt someone."

"Yeah, G," he said. "I'll go have a word with them."

At that moment, Charlie Horse was clearing her lane when one of the boys hit the pins on the adjacent alley. One of them crossed over and hit her hard on the elbow. She let out a big, "Owww!" and pulled back into the cave. I asked her if she was okay, and although she was fighting back tears, she said, "I think so. I can still move it."

The boys out front were enthusiastically laughing and pushing each other over what they had done.

I didn't quite know how I might take on three older boys, but I was mad enough to not be thinking straight. I started through the opening to the lane, but Borneo grabbed the back of my pants. "I got a better idea, G. Watch this. Danny, grab me one of those old balls back in the corner."

Borneo returned the ball the boys were using with a little backspin so it wouldn't quite make it to the end of the ball return. As one of the boys stepped on to the alley to retrieve the ball, Borneo let the second ball fly down the lane. The boy managed to sidestep the ball and glared at the end of the alley.

"Let's hope he gets the message," Borneo said. "G, you take over for Charlie Horse. And watch yourself." He turned to Sally and asked, "You okay? We can take you to the hospital if you want."

She replied, "I'm okay. It will be a little bruised tomorrow, but everything seems to be working."

The boys rolled a couple of normal frames, but then double-balled Albert, just like they had Crackers.

"I guess they don't learn," Borneo said. "Well, here goes our tip."

He reached under one of the planks and pulled out a jar of petroleum jelly. "If this doesn't send the right message, I don't know what will." He then proceeded to coat the inside of the thumb holes with the grease and rolled the balls back up the lane. The boys were laughing uncontrollably when they took the balls from the return. Borneo could see that they were lining up to send two balls down the lane at once.

"C'mon, Charlie Horse. Take a look at this," Borneo said.

We all moved to the lane where the boys were bowling. They approached the foul line, swung their arms back, and both balls went flying backwards. One of them landed directly on the foot of one of the girls, while the other hit the third boy directly in the groin. The girl let out a large scream, protesting that her foot was broken. All three girls started berating the two boys who lost their grips.

We were back in the cave having a good laugh of our own. "Where did you learn that trick?" I asked Borneo.

"You can't use it too often," he replied, "but every once in a while, it sends just the right message."

The girls were still all over the boys, who were protesting they didn't have any idea what could have happened.

Borneo said, "C'mon. Let's go finish taking care of these guys."

Six pin boys started up the alley, led by Borneo. When we were about halfway up, the group turned their anger at us, yelling that we were trying to kill them. The commotion brought Yakky and Frank to the lane.

One of the greaser boys turned to Frank and said, "These guys did something to the balls that made them fly out of our hands. It broke my girlfriend's foot, and look at my friend."

The boy who had been hit in the groin was sitting on the bench, ashen faced and groaning.

Borneo said, "They were double-balling and using the light balls with the light pins. Charlie Horse could have gotten hurt pretty bad. I don't know what happened to those balls, but the way they were screwing around, I wouldn't be surprised if it was just some prank they messed up."

Frank looked over at Charlie Horse holding her elbow. He turned back to the boys and said, "That right?"

The biggest one said, "No, we were just bowling. We were just having some fun. These guys were the ones trying to hurt us."

Frank looked at me. "What do you say, G?"

"I say they were trying to hurt us. If one of them got hurt instead, serves 'em right."

Frank turned to the group. "Well, that's that then. G says you started it, then you started it. He don't tell no lies. You boys turn in your shoes and leave. And maybe don't think about coming back."

"You can't throw us out. We'll leave when we are done bowling."

Albert and Borneo started moving toward the boys. I followed them. The boy on the bench said, "Hey, let's get out of this two-bit hole in the wall. There's places that know how to treat paying customers."

The girls said, "Yeah, screw them. They're all losers anyway. Just a bunch of misfits who can't do no better in life than work in a stinking bowling alley."

I was the one who responded. "I'm proud to be a pin boy, and I'm proud to work with these guys...and Charlie Horse. I'll take these people you call losers and misfits any day of the week over you. Now get out before we show you how tough pin boys really are."

Frank said, "You heard him. Get out and stay out."

When they had left the building, Frank said, "Now I'll never get finished with my paper. Why don't all of you take off so I can read without any interruption. I guess we're closing early tonight."

Sally came up to me and said, "C'mon, Gianni. Walk me home. It's been a long day."

CHAPTER 14

"Jacky, paisan, come sta?"

"Tony! Bene, my friend. Everything is just fine. I'm sure you're calling me with good news."

"How long have you known me?" Tony asked. "Have I ever failed to come through in the clutch? Didn't you always say, when something needs to get done, call Tony Gallo?"

"That's what I always said. I guess it's still true."

Jacky Di Felipo and Tony Gallo were two of a kind when it came to maneuvering people. But while Tony was more inclined to use his intimidating physical presence, the slightly built Jacky relied on his ability to talk anyone to death. Still, usually both men got what they were looking for.

"So is everything set on your end, Tony?" Di Felipo asked.

"Well, I got a little bit more prep work to do, but you get your boy to agree to stop here in Riverbend, and we'll make it worth his while. Let me tell you, Jacky, I'm planning a party like you ain't never seen before. We're gonna have everything but Garibaldi's redshirts."

"Then I guess we better get down to business. We get a grand upfront, and we keep that whether or not PG wins, although he ain't lost in three years. Plus, when we win, we get whatever the prize money is. 'Course, that ain't where the real money's made. It's the side bets and the merchandise where we clean up. It's a real shame, you know. P. G. Peckham is the best bowler in the world, and he still can't make enough money playing in tournaments to keep himself fixed up. If he doesn't go on these barnstorming tours, he wouldn't be able to live no better than a common laborer. You know, last year, he made fifty grand on the tour, and he was the top earner. I know that sounds like good money, but after travel expenses, alimony, and entertainment, if you know what I mean, he barely had enough to keep him in cheap scotch. Plus, his idiot ex-brother-in-law got him into some screwy land deal, and now we got the IRS breathing down our necks. So we travel the country taking on the local talent. I set it up, he knocks 'em down, so to speak."

Tony said, "No problem with the thousand bucks. We'll have a check cut to you by the end of the week."

"That's great, Tony. PG's thinking about doing a tour late August, early September, before any of the big tournaments."

"Perfect. I was thinking Labor Day. We'll play up the working class guy angle. And don't worry about the publicity. We'll have everyone but the Pope turned out to meet him. We'll have a huge clambake during the day and the match of the century that night."

Di Felipo said, "I know you'll take care of things, Tony. By the way, where are we holding the match?"

"That's one of the best parts," Tony replied. "We're having it at Riverbend Alleys. It's this old place built by the Mick who started the Wortham Broom Company for his wife and kids. It would almost be an historical building if it wasn't such a rundown piece of crap. Anyway, none of it is automatic. They still use human pin boys. It'll be an old time grudge match. Whadda ya think, Jacky?"

Di Felipo thought he might be able to play Tony a little on the pin boy angle. "I don't know, Tony. I don't know if PG ever bowled where there were pin boys."

"That ain't the least of his worries, Jacky. He'll be bowling against Riverbend's best. Marcus Aurelius Pandolfo, also known as Mingo."

"You're a crack up, Tony," Di Felipo said. "You think maybe I should have PG wear a coonskin cap?"

"Don't laugh. It might be a good idea. Let me tell you, Jacky. Mingo's good enough that he's gonna beat your guy."

"Hey, we'll see about that. Like I said, PG hasn't lost in three years."

Tony's voice took a very serious tone. "I'm not sure I made myself as clear as I should have. Mingo's gonna beat your guy. It can be close, but Peckham loses."

Di Felipo paused a moment. "Are you serious, *goombah*? PG won't throw a match. I can't talk him into that."

Tony laughed out loud. "Jacky, you could talk the Pope into converting to Protestant if you put your mind on it. But I don't expect you guys to do it for nothing. How much do you usually clear on one of these stops after expenses? Three, maybe four grand?"

Jacky thought four grand would have been spectacular, but said, "Four grand would be a bad night, Tony. Hell, we played smaller towns than yours and cleared six easy."

Tony thought, *Be careful here, Jacky, you're not playing with just any small town hick.* But at least he was still plenty below the number Tony had in mind. "Well, how does ten thousand clear sound? Think you could get PG to break his streak for that kind of cash?"

"How you gonna get ten grand?" Jacky asked.

"Simple. You're gonna bet the farm on Mingo."

"Tony, I'm glad you're my friend. I wouldn't wish you as an enemy on anyone."

"Jacky, my boy, if you can't make money with your friends, who can you make it with?"

"Let me talk to PG," Jacky said. "I'll get back to you in the next day or two."

Tony Gallo smiled to himself. Things couldn't be working out better. Not only would he get to save the city—his city—but he'd make a few bucks in the process. "I'll talk to you then, Jacky. *Ciao.*"

CHAPTER 15

Jacky Di Felipo wondered why anyone would want to visit Buffalo, much less live there. He remembered the old joke, Buffalo only has two seasons—winter and fourth of July. No matter how bad people said the weather was, Jacky thought, it was probably worse. Unfortunately, Buffalo was where P. G. Peckham called home. Jacky hated leaving New York City. Going west through the Lincoln Tunnel always left him feeling uncomfortable and out of his natural element. But this was a situation that couldn't be handled over the phone. First, he had to loosen up PG with some Chivas Regal, and then he had to ease PG into seeing the merit to the plan. PG could be a disagreeable sort for no better reason than he thought bowlers didn't get the publicity and respect other star athletes got. Yeah, Jacky mused, this was going to take time and the telephone just wasn't an option. Nobody could refuse Jacky looking him right in the face. Besides, the personal touch is what endeared Jacky to all his "clients."

Jacky's shiny red Cadillac DeVille was a great car on the open road. It was smooth and powerful and quiet, handling road bumps like it was stepping over an egg. He got to exit 50 on the Thruway in just under seven hours, pretty good time really. Jacky made sure he didn't push the Caddy too hard—that big red boat was an inviting target for the state police who patrolled the sticks, which as far as he was concerned was anyplace north or west of the Tappan Zee. They loved nothing better than to hassle slick city guys driving expensive cars. And they couldn't be bought either. Keep your mouth shut, take the ticket, and curse the bastard once he was out of sight.

Jacky had mostly been a small operator in New York City. A little numbers running and loan sharking kept him floating but not entirely comfortable. He knew some of the right people—he could get expensive suits and shoes straight from the docks—but he was mostly seen as a guy who was never going to make his bones in the heavyweight division.

That was until this professional bowling deal fell in his lap. All the bowlers on the tour needed the extra money that came with exhibition matches, and not one of them was enough of a businessman to work the deals without some help. Jacky's first client was a tall, skinny Brooklyn kid named Anthony Carter. Carter was temporarily dating the daughter of Giuseppe Simone, a brutish *capo* from the lower east side of Manhattan. Normally, the idea of one of his daughters dating a non-Italian would have made Simone unhappy, but while he loved his daughter very much, he recognized that she wasn't going to win any beauty contests. Plus, it had been a few years since she could wiggle into a size 12. The Italian boys who went out with her were mostly trying to ingratiate themselves to Simone. At least Carter seemed to actually like his daughter for who she was, not who he was.

When Giuseppe Simone threw a birthday party for his daughter at the *Tre Famiglia* restaurant, Anthony Carter and Jacky Di Felipo both found themselves on the fringes of the party. Once they started talking, they also found they shared a mutual passion for making money. Carter had hustled a little at places along the Jersey shore, but it was dangerous to hustle strangers, especially when he couldn't make much more than fifty or a hundred bucks a night.

He knew barnstorming could bring some big money, but he had no idea how to make it work. He mentioned it to Jacky, and Jacky said, "Don't worry about the details, kid. I'll call you and tell you when and where, and you just show up and bowl. Whatever we make, we split 50-50."

Carter thought about it for a moment and said, "How about 60-40. You get the 40."

Jacky said, "How about I tell Don Simone what a good kid you are and we make it 50-50."

Carter thought 50-50 was a pretty good deal to have Giuseppe Simone on your side. He never thought going out with his daughter would work out so well. Besides, once he was established, he could dictate whatever terms he wanted to Jacky. "Deal," he said. They shook hands, downed a shot of Sambuca, and silently congratulated themselves on being so fortunate.

Things were pretty good for about a year. Jacky was a natural hustler, especially when it came to the rubes who hung out in bowling alleys. The first thing he did was give Carter some lessons on shearing the sheep, as he called it.

"You can't sucker a mark if he doesn't think he has a chance," Jacky said. "And he ain't gonna think he has a chance if you start throwing nothing but strikes from the first frame. You gotta keep him and the crowd into the match. You gotta remember, this guy thinks he coulda been a pro bowler if only his old lady wasn't such a nag about a regular paycheck every week.

"He's got something to prove to himself and all his buddies. You don't want him to be afraid of you. You want him to think it's his night. So he starts falling behind, you maybe miss a spare. Make him think you're just human, not some sort of bowling machine. Then, right when he thinks he's got you, then you slam the door on him. Nothing hurts worse than having someone snatch away your glory. Meanwhile, I'll be in the crowd seeing if I can get some of the local yokels to back their boy with some cash. Ain't nobody gonna bet if they see you're gonna blitz him from the start."

Their first tour together was during the summer on Long Island and the Jersey shore. Carter bowled well, winning all but one match. By the time it was over, Jacky had cleared close to twenty thousand mostly tax-free dollars. Carter returned to the pro bowling circuit in the fall. Jacky made it his business to drop by to see him at some of the stops close to New York. This gave him the opportunity to meet some of the other pro bowlers who figured Jacky could do for them what he did for Carter. Pretty quickly, he had a small stable of barnstorming bowlers and an annual income approaching six figures.

Jacky started earning a comfortable living, and he even noticed some of the men who wouldn't even offer him a quick *buon giorno* before were being much friendlier. Jacky knew that in their business, money bought lots of things, especially friendship. Things could hardly have been better for Jacky.

It was at a tour stop in Philadelphia when P. G. Peckham approached him. While most of the bowlers on the tour were duller than dry white toast, Peckham was a bundle of energy and showmanship. After releasing the ball, he would grind his hips like some keggling Elvis Presley, almost as if he was guiding the rolling sphere with his gyrations. His signature move after bowling a strike was to turn to his opponent and pretend to shoot him with his index fingers, artfully finishing the scene by blowing the unseen smoke from the tip of each finger and holstering them in his front pockets. Day or night, he was rarely without his bright, blue-tinted sunglasses, the round kind favored by the flower children whose pictures appeared regularly in *Time* magazine. His pants were meticulously tailored and just a bit too strategically tight, and his shirts would have to be toned down to only be called loud. His most brazen habit was talking to the crowd and his opponent, often peppering the match with comments like, "If you can't deck 'em, you won't beat Peckham," and "I'm on a real roll now, ladies and gentlemen." In the gentlemanly sport of tenpins, this type of obnoxious arrogance was unheard of. It was not surprising that most of the other bowlers despised and envied Peckham at the same time.

Peckham was certainly the only one who had real groupies waiting for him after a match. They weren't quite as good-looking or wild as rock star groupies, but they were at least as enthusiastic.

Peckham was a little man, not more than five foot six in his bowling shoes, with hair trying to decide between red and brown that he tried to push straight back on his head. Unfortunately, no matter how much hair tonic he used, it still had a tendency to spring straight up like a bed of spikes pointing to the ceiling. He didn't weigh more than 135 pounds, but he compensated for his slightness by having a right arm that would have made Popeye envious. Somehow, he threw a sixteen-pound bowling ball like it had no more mass than a tennis ball.

Peckham had been the top bowler on the tour for three years straight, mostly owing to the fact that when he wasn't in bed with a woman or drinking scotch, he was practicing his craft.

The best kept secret in bowling was that P. G. Peckham out-practiced all the other bowlers. He bowled three hundred games with an astonishing regularity, so often that he insisted the initials PG stood for "Perfect Game" instead of Pierre Gaston, the name given to him by his French-Canadian mother. He wasn't even sure anyone besides his family and his ex-wives knew his real name, and he was paying all of them plenty to keep their mouths shut.

Peckham was a barnstorming dream come true. Arrogant to the point where people would bet against him just because they didn't like him, a natural performer, and as consistent as anyone who ever threw a bowling ball. Jacky had a good thing going with Peckham, and he had to make sure nothing—not even Tony Gallo's overinflated ego—came between him and his meal ticket.

Fifteen minutes after paying the Thruway toll, Jacky pulled up to Peckham's house, a small, olive green two-family dwelling built in the early 1950s. It wasn't in Buffalo proper but a well-mannered suburb named Amherst, just a short distance from the main campus of the University of Buffalo. Peckham lived in the upstairs flat and rented the downstairs to a couple of girls who occasionally didn't mind bartering for the rent.

Jacky rang the bell and waited, ringing twice more before a bleary-eyed P. G. Peckham answered. He was dressed in boxer shorts with a pattern of ten bowling pins being scattered by a ball decorating the front, a black T-shirt and calf-length black socks. His hair pointed skyward and his blue granny glasses hid what were probably the bloodshot effects of a night that ended closer to dawn than dusk.

"Jacky?" Peckham gurgled. "What the hell are you doing in Buffalo?"

"Come to see you, Peege. We got business to talk about. You gonna invite me inside?"

Peckham tried his best to act alert, but the Scotch was still winning the battle for his brain. "Sure, Jacky. C'mon up. You can help me look for the coffee."

Thirty five minutes later, a semi-cleaned up Peckham sat down at the kitchen table with Jacky. "So you came all the way to Buffalo just to talk business? What happened? New York forget to pay its phone bill?"

"I got you a first class gig. In Riverbend."

"Where is Riverbend?" Peckham asked.

"Between Utica and Albany. Closer to Albany."

"Fine, but why come all the way up here to tell me. You could have called. I would have answered the phone, eventually."

Jacky thought it was as good a time as any to start the hard sell. "It's a great place. It's this old bowling alley, built before 1900 even. And get this. They don't have automatic machines for anything. It's all pin boys. Old time bowling. DiNobilis, liquor, and tenpins.

"Like I said, Jacky, I can bowl anywhere. Nobody on the planet can beat P. G. Peckham, not without some sort of handicap. Just tell me when to show up."

"Labor Day weekend. There'll be a celebration to make George Meany himself proud."

"That'll work out great for me," Peckham said. "It's been a while since I did the Thruway tour. You got Rochester and Syracuse lined up? And don't forget Kingston. I have…a good friend in Kingston."

"Most of the details are worked out," Jacky said. "You'll start in Buffalo on the fifteenth of August—that's a Thursday—and work your way down to Yonkers. Fourteen days, ten matches, four to six grand clear for us each time, assuming of course you win. Not a bad couple of weeks, eh?"

"I can hardly wait. Two weeks of living out of my suitcase and eating at greasy spoons."

"We're only hitting the big towns this time," Jacky said. "The money should be pretty good all around. After Yonkers, it's back to Riverbend. These hicks are just gonna love you."

"What the hell is so special about Riverbend? Ten matches in two weeks is plenty for me."

"It's special," Jacky said, "because it's gonna be the biggest payday on the tour. Ten grand. And you don't even have to win."

"What do you mean I don't have to win? We make most of our money getting the locals to bet on their boy. And how are we going to make more money there than the big towns? That don't make no sense."

Jacky gave Peckham a minute to let things sink in. "Actually, PG, what I mean is that we get the ten grand when you don't win."

Peckham blinked rapidly, like he was trying to flutter the fuzziness from his eyes. "I may still be half drunk, Jacky, but did you say I'm going to lose? That's not gonna happen, Jacky. Peckham don't lose to anyone especially on purpose."

"PG, sometimes you gotta give a little to get a lot. Look, you had to lose sooner or later. Once somebody beats you, any other time you lose ain't gonna be no big deal. But this first time, this guy's gonna be a hero, a legend. They call this guy Mingo after that Daniel Boone Indian guy. And all you have to do is shake his hand and walk away with the money."

Peckham sat speechless at the table. Jacky thought, if this guy starts thinking too hard, he might blow a fuse.

Jacky said, "You want a Chivas?"

Peckham looked up. "No, but I think there's some OJ in the icebox and some vodka in the freezer. I think I could use a pick me up."

Jacky mixed the screwdriver in a good size tumbler, lots of vodka, a little ice, and enough orange juice to make it official. Peckham gulped half the drink, leaned back, hit his chest with the side of his fist, and belched. "You're nuts, Jacky," he said.

Jacky did his best to adopt a soothing tone. "Haven't I always done right by you? Haven't you and me made more money in the last couple of years than anyone else on the tour? Listen, Peege, now ain't the time to go all indignant on me. Now's the time to think about what's important. Money. What do you think is gonna happen when this guy beats you? I'll tell you what's gonna happen. Every two-bit league bowler with a 200 average is gonna be calling me up begging me for a match. Think about it. P. G. Peckham gets beat by some nobody. Now all the nobodys think they can be the next. You see what I mean?"

Peckham downed the rest of the screwdriver. "I get you, Jacky. But it ain't in me to lose on purpose."

Jacky saw Peckham decompress a little. "I know. Tell you what. Don't just throw the match. Make him beat you. Make him throw a strike at the right time. I'm just saying open the door a crack and let him find his own way in."

Peckham sighed. "You're right, Jacky. Two weeks after it's over, I'll still be P. G. Peckham, the greatest bowler who ever lived. And maybe I'll just have a rematch with Wingo or Dingo or whatever his name is and kick his tail."

"That's my boy," Jacky said. "You won't regret this, PG. Not for a second. Now what do you say we go someplace classy for a drink, my treat."

Peckham immediately perked up. "I know just the place. Frank's Cassanova on Bailey. There's this dancer there named Joanie, does this thing with some glow-in-the-dark tassels that you won't believe."

"Sounds perfect, Peege. Just perfect."

CHAPTER 16

It was a little after noon and everyone was still at the front of the lanes. Albert was sleeping so loudly we thought about putting the cotton in our ears. Borneo was reading a paperback by some guy name Nietzsche, who Vinnie told me was a linebacker for the Packers. Vinnie and I were teaching Charlie Horse how to play the card game pitch. Danny was sitting at one of the benches watching the second hand sweep past the digits on his Timex. Without warning, a large group of young children with energy to spare burst through the door. Danny turned to us and yelled, "Duckpins!"

Vinnie said to me, "I was going out on that hand. I had high, low, jack, and game."

Charlie Horse said, "Yeah, you could have been the pitch champion of Riverbend Alleys."

Danny took off down the alley, disappeared into the cave, and momentarily reappeared through the alley opening. He looked at Vinnie and me, held one up, and again said, "Duckpins."

Borneo put his football book in his pocket and walked over to us. He said, "It's kids from the YMCA day camp. Couple of times each summer, they bring them over here to bowl. It's a fun day today, boys. Duckpins is easy work."

Yakky came over and said, "Remember when I told you there are three kinds of pins? Duckpins is the third. They're the same as regular pins except a lot smaller in size. Put them on the same spots. They don't use regular bowling balls either. They use this smaller ball, like the size of a bocce ball, with no holes in it. It's great for little kids who don't have enough power to throw a real ball and knock down the heavy pins. Same guy who takes care of our pins makes the

Duckpins. When we decide a pin ain't good anymore, we give it to that guy, and he whittles it into a duckpin."

"Let's go, boys," Borneo said.

"What about the pay and the tips?" Vinnie asked. "How does that work?"

"We don't worry too much about score and games with these kids," Yakky said. "We'll let them bowl about an hour, and we charge a buck and a half a kid. Alley keeps a buck, pin boys get the fifty cents."

Borneo was right. The kids seemed to be having a great time, although the camp counselors were running from one lane to the next making sure the kids were rolling the balls in the right direction. It was a lot easier for us. The pins were lighter, and they were easier to handle, and the noise was hardly loud enough for us to need our ear cotton.

Vinnie said, "This looks like a gas, G. What do you say we come in early one morning and give it a shot."

"Why not," I responded. "I can't be any worse than I am at regular bowling."

"Well, G," Vinnie said, "some of us are good at one thing, and some of us are good at everything. I can't wait to try this."

The kids bowled about an hour and a half, leaving with about as much energy as when they came in. Danny put the Duckpins away, and we all went back to the front. Albert told Borneo he was going for a walk, and Borneo told him to make sure he was back in time for the Pro League. He assured Borneo he would be back in plenty of time.

Albert returned a few minutes late, and Borneo gave him a stern look, but Albert just grinned his odd grin and got ready to do his work. Things went pretty normally and no team threatened the 4,000 pin mark.

Toward the end of the night, a very large man in a sharp, gray suit walked into the bowling alley. Most of the bowlers stopped to shake hands with him, and he seemed to revel in all the attention he was receiving. He walked over to Mingo, said something in his ear, and then sat down. He rummaged through his pockets and found a DiNobili, lit it, and settled in on the bowlers bench.

"Who is the fat guy?" I asked no one in particular.

Vinnie answered, "It's a guy named Tony Gallo. He used to come into Paulie's place all the time. I don't know who he is exactly, but he seemed pretty important. He got a lot of respect from everyone in the back room."

Borneo said, "Tony Gallo is officially the director of public works, but in reality he runs Riverbend. He's the big *goombah* in town and has been for as long as I can remember."

I looked out through the alley, and for a moment, it seemed like Tony Gallo focused on my face, nodding at me almost imperceptibly. The bowlers finished up the night, packed up their balls, once more shook Tony Gallo's hand, and left the alley, leaving only Mingo and Tony at the head of the lane. Tony had his back to us, but I could see his massive right arm around Mingo's slight shoulders, his left hand moving animatedly back and forth, like he was conducting a band. After about ten minutes, Tony released his hold on Mingo, patted him vigorously on the back, and marched out of the building. Mingo hesitated a minute, picked up his ball bag, and started to leave. He looked down at his shoes and realized he hadn't changed into his street shoes. He slowly slipped off the bowling shoes and laced up a pair of shiny, oxblood, wingtip cordovans. He left the alley looking like he was carrying the weight of Riverbend on his shoulders.

Little did we know at the time that was almost exactly what he was doing.

CHAPTER 17

Mingo left Riverbend Alleys wondering why Tony Gallo picked him. He wasn't connected. He was just one of the neighborhood bums, a kid never likely to be much more than what he was at that moment. Sure, he was a good bowler—everybody knew that—but a match against P. G. Peckham, the greatest bowler in the world? He was trying to figure out what the catch was.

Mingo didn't like the idea of dealing with Tony Gallo. The man scared him. Everybody knew Tony ran Riverbend, and nobody who ever tangled with Tony came out on top. But this was his big chance. His opportunity to prove that maybe he wasn't a nobody from a nowhere town.

He allowed himself to drift off with that thought. What if he, Marcus Aurelius Pandolfo, beat the greatest bowler of all time? Why, they would probably give him a PBA tour card right then and there. He could make twenty or thirty or even fifty thousand dollars a year, just like Peckham. In Riverbend, he'd be lucky to ever make six thousand dollars a year. Women would look at him with dreamy eyes, instead of a nasty glare. The people at Teddy's Tavern would buy him drinks just for the privilege of hearing about how he beat the invincible Peckham.

"Yeah," Mingo thought, "I would be set for life. I could bust out of this rathole of a city and walk into the biggest towns in the country like I owned them. The girls would call out, 'Over here, Mingo,' and 'You're the greatest, Mingo.' I'd be somebody, a big shot, a star."

Maybe he shouldn't care why Tony Gallo picked him. This was his chance. P. G. Peckham would be at his bowling alley, the place where he knew every board on every lane. He would bowl against P. G. Peckham. He would bowl against him and beat him.

In the morning, he would tell Tony Gallo to print up the flyers and get an article in the *Daily Current*. Riverbend was the place where P. G. Peckham would meet his match.

CHAPTER 18

It was another miserable day in August. I heard someone called it the dog days. It was years before I realized it didn't have anything to do with dogs, but the appearance of Sirius, the dog star. Some ancient misunderstanding about where all the heat comes from. Frank had a fan in his office, but the rest of the bowling alley was oppressively hot. It was rare for someone to show up to bowl on a dog day afternoon.

Danny and Crackers stayed inside just in case someone did show up. Albert had the day off. Vinnie was trying to show Charlie Horse how to play pitch. Better him than me. She pretty much had no sense for cards. I walked down by the river and found Borneo sitting on the bank, drinking an orange soda.

"Mind if I sit with you, Borneo?" I asked.

"It's a free country, G-man," he said. "I guess that means you can sit wherever you want."

"How did you get the nickname Borneo?"

"Not the way most people think, because of my hair," he said. "It came from my little brother. My real name is Bruno. He had a hard time pronouncing it, and it sounded like Borneo."

"Bruno like the wrestler guy, Bruno Sammartino? He's the best wrestler ever. I love watching wrestling on TV on Sunday. I especially like it when Bruno speaks in Italian. My parents don't speak in Italian very much, except when they don't want us to understand something. But I still know some words and can follow a little."

"I guess, but I was born way before he became the best known Italian since Joe DiMaggio. I was named for my grandfather, Bruno Rocca. The name means brown stone or something like that. That's me. A brown stone. If I fell in the river, I would sink like a brown stone." Borneo laughed. "You know what one of the shortest books in the world is? Famous Italian Swimmers."

"What made you decide to become a pin boy, Borneo?"

"I was looking to make a career move after I got out of the army."

I looked at him.

"Not really," he said. Then he stared out across the river. "Maybe it's time to tell somebody how I became a pin boy."

And then he just started talking.

"I wasn't much at school. I almost dropped out but managed to get my diploma from Most Precious Blood. Seems nobody was allowed to drop out of Catholic School. Couple of months after my eighteenth birthday, I got a notice from the local draft board. I was to report for my physical, see if I was army material. No surprise. Four months later, I was in basic training. Soon as that was done, I was off to Vietnam.

"It was Christmas day, 1966. We had been in the Kim Son Valley for most of that year. I was with the First Cavalry Division. I was in Company C, Charlie Company. First Battalion, Twelfth Cavalry. I never did quite understand all the parts, so if someone asked who I was with, I usually just said First Cav. I got there in February and saw my first action right away. Operation White Wing they called it. Day and night we pounded the NVA. We dropped bombs, we dropped napalm. We shot at them with big guns, machine guns, rifles. Hell, we even used BZ grenades. BZ was a drug, like LSD, only a lot stronger. They said the effects of BZ could last for weeks, maybe even affect you for the rest of your life. Lot of us wondered if it might not be better to drop some of those BZ grenades close enough so we could breathe some in.

"I didn't know why that piece of ground was so important. But it didn't matter if I understood anything. It was drilled into me that I was a trained killer. Imagine feeling proud to be known as a trained killer. And I was proud. Anyway, they said we killed over a thousand of their regulars in the operation. Six weeks exactly and a thousand nameless, faceless men. The enemy, if you believed what you read in the papers. It wasn't easy to see how we were saving the world from godless communism by killing everyone we could. So we spent the rest of the year trying to keep what we took. By Christmas, I was a hard-boiled, veteran soldier.

"There was a ceasefire for the Christmas holiday, but for most of us, it just felt like another day. They gave us a special meal of some processed meat that was supposed to pass for turkey and some watery potatoes with lumpy gravy. We ate it like it was real home cooking. Some guys sang Christmas carols. White Christmas in Vietnam. Good joke.

"The day after Christmas, it rained on and off. By night, the rain clouds were scattered, and we could actually see the moon peeking through the clouds. Most of us had gotten sick with stomach cramps. Probably from the special Christmas dinner they put together.

"We were guarding the northern perimeter of Landing Zone Bird—LZ's we called them—about two hundred yards from the Kim Son River. There were about twenty of us, maybe half new replacements anxious to see their first action. About one in the morning, they got their chance. We heard machine guns chattering, and then someone started yelling that the NVA had breached the perimeter. Right about then, the clouds parted and the bright moon made it easy to see what must have been hundreds of NVA coming at us, single file. At that moment, I figured I was dead. Two of our guys started firing their machine guns and were able to hold off the charge long enough for the sergeant to grab a few guys to form a new perimeter. I moved back toward the main trench that we used as the fire direction center. Some of the NVA started jumping over the trench, and as they did, I fired my rifle at them. One of the NVA got into the trench and started running at me, screaming in Vietnamese. He had a knife in his left hand, gun in the other. I had plenty of time to point my rifle at him and pull the trigger, but when I did, nothing happened.

"When he was almost on top of me, I threw the rifle at him with me right behind. He managed to deflect the rifle but that gave me enough time to jump on him. He made a wild slash and caught me just under my arm, pulling down to my hip. There was lots of blood, but they told me the wound wasn't all that deep. Still needed a hundred stitches to close.

"I fell back, and he raised the gun that was still in his right hand. Just as he was pulling the trigger, someone shot him in the back of the head. He got the round off, but his aim was disrupted enough that he hit me in my upper right chest. The bullet passed through, somehow not catching anything vital. I started to poke my head above the trench when I heard one of the sergeants yell at us to get down. Then I heard this sound like a million bees flying overhead, and this horrible screaming. They had fired a beehive at the NVA line, a shell that fired thousands of small metal arrows. Dozens of NVA soldiers were lying there, their bodies torn to shreds by the arrows. I had never seen anything like it. I was close to losing consciousness, but I still threw up.

"Next thing I remembered was someone yelling for a medic. A totally naked man appears with supplies and bandages. He puts pressure on the wounds and starts asking me questions, like what is my name, and where am I from, and where is Riverbend, New York. I asked him why he was naked, and he said he was asleep when the fighting started and didn't have time to dress. I started thinking, this isn't really happening. I'm in a dream where there are ghostly NVA regulars dancing through the moonlight, and bees attacking them, and naked medics trying to repair the wounded. I think I started laughing, and then coughing, and then crying. The medic gave me a shot of something, and the next thing I remember, I woke up in a hospital in Saigon.

"They told me later the whole battle only lasted an hour. Fifty-eight guys from the First Cav got killed, seventy-seven wounded. A bunch of guys got medals. They said we got a few hundred NVA. That was the thing I could never understand. How could we kill five of them for every one of us, but every day they still kept coming at us. This puny little country had an endless supply of their own trained killers.

"Eventually, the wounds from the knife and the bullet healed. But I couldn't get the sight of those NVA soldiers lying there, shredded from the beehive, out of my head. I mean, why should

I care. Nobody in the company thought they were human anyway. But their screams woke me every night anyway. Most nights, they still do."

He turned to me and smiled. "I haven't had a full night's sleep in a year and a half," he said.

"I finished my tour guarding some supply warehouse. I came back to the states through San Francisco. There were people with signs that said things like 'Baby Killer' and 'Stop the War Machine' and 'Peace.' I mean, it wasn't my war. In the end, I fought for my buddies, not Lyndon Johnson or the government.

"And then I wondered what was left for me. I didn't hate the war, I didn't hate America, I didn't hate anything. I just didn't care. I didn't care where I went or what I did. So I came back to Riverbend. If you don't care, Riverbend is not a bad place to be. For a couple of weeks, I just stayed in my room at my parents' house. I read a little, grew my hair, and tried to sleep. On the first warm day of spring, I went outside and walked. I went from one end of the town to the other. I walked down to the river and sat on the bank for a while. Same place we are now.

"When I got up to leave, I saw Riverbend Alleys, and there was a sign in the window, 'Pin Boys Wanted.' What the hell, I thought. And here I am. That's how I became a pin boy."

I wasn't sure what to say. I didn't know much about Vietnam or the war, except what I saw on the news. I guess I believed what I was told by the president. Borneo made me think things weren't always what the man of the TV said.

"So you can't swim?" I said.

"No, I can't swim," he answered.

"Are you going to be a pin boy the rest of your life?"

He turned at me and smiled. "Until something better comes along," he said.

I stood up and brushed some of the dirt off my pants. "I think I'll go back and see how Vinnie and Charlie Horse are doing."

Borneo said, "I'll catch you in a few minutes."

I took two steps toward the bowling alley and turned back to Borneo. "You think there are a lot of guys like you? Guys who came back from the war with bad things in their heads."

"Probably so, G-man," he said.

"Maybe you should find them and talk with them. Just so they can let you know you aren't all by yourself," I said.

"I might just do that," he said.

CHAPTER 19

It was three in the afternoon, and David Greene was getting ready for the Wednesday night city men's golf league by putting into an overturned glass. In twenty minutes, he had made only two putts. The private line on his desk rang just as he was in his backswing, and as he swung forward, he missed the putt completely. He knew the call could only be from his wife or Tony Gallo, neither of whom made him feel like answering.

He picked up the phone. "Mayor Greene."

"What's with all the formality, Davey? It's me, Tony."

"Hey, Tony, what's shaking?"

"You playing in the men's league tonight?" Tony asked.

"Yeah, I can't wait to get out there. My putting has been on fire. I wouldn't be surprised if I won the prize for fewest putts, you know."

"What do you say you play with me this afternoon, Davey? We have lots to talk about."

He felt caught between a rock and a hard place. Either he had to play with Tony or with his miserable District Attorney brother-in-law, the much despised Elliot Levine. Elliot made no secret of his ambition to seek higher office, and he wasn't above flexing the muscle of the DA's office to help him along. Elliot didn't have friends as much as he had acquaintances who could help his career. There was even a time when Elliot investigated Tony Gallo, although for some reason, he gave up on the idea almost as soon as he started. From that point forward, an uneasy truce seemed to exist between Elliot and Tony, best illustrated by the disingenuous affection they showed for each other in public. Greene thought at least he could get a little dig in at Tony.

"I don't know, Tony," he said. "I'm supposed to play with Elliot today."

"Hey, how is that hell-raiser Elliot doing anyway?" Tony asked. The enthusiasm in his voice sounded genuine. That scared Greene even more.

"Oh, you know. Making Riverbend safer for all of us."

"He's the best, ain't he?" Tony said.

"Yeah, and a first rate hacker too."

"Don't worry about Elliot, Davey. I'll arrange everything. Besides, Elliot needs to talk with Tom Pagliarulo. They caught his kid shoplifting at Newberry's. He's a good kid, just a little rambunctious. I'll see you out there." Tony hung up abruptly. Greene tried three more putts and never even scared the glass. *Who needs this?* he thought.

The golf course was the pride and joy of Tony Gallo. As public works director, it was under his direct supervision, and he would just as soon cancel garbage pick-ups as see a weed in a fairway. The course was built in 1930, two years after Tony started working for Riverbend.

He remembered his mentor, Bobby Cahill, taking him along to walk the wooded area just beyond the city limits where the course would be built. "It don't look like much now, Tony, but when we're done, this golf course will be the envy of every burg from here to Kingston. People will drive fifty miles just to play Riverbend Municipal Golf Course. Just remember one thing, Tony. You got a jewel like this, you polish it and take care of it every day. You take care of it, and it will take care of you."

Eight years later, Bobby Cahill was shot in bed by the man whose wife was deliriously singing his praises as a lover only moments earlier. By that time, Tony had become Cahill's right hand man and confidant. The day after it happened, Tony remembered thinking, "It wasn't such a good idea that you had to brag to me about your skill in the bedroom, was it, Bobby? Otherwise, I might never have known to anonymously call that man and tell him he better get home quick because it sounded like his wife was being strangled by someone."

The man rushed home, colt pistol in hand, expecting to find someone raping his wife. He crashed through the front door at about the same time as his wife was letting out a pretty fair imitation of Tarzan's primal cry. He flew up the stairs three at a time, and when he burst into the bedroom, he shot first and asked questions later. The coroner determined that mere seconds before the fateful shot, Cahill was climaxing, causing him to consider listing the cause of death as "shot while shooting."

Tony, of course, learned a valuable lesson from Bobby Cahill. Never tell anyone whose wife you are banging. And if someone finds out, move on elsewhere. There's plenty of women to love, but you only get one life.

Tony sent the biggest arrangement of flowers to the funeral home, making sure everyone saw the inscription, "In Memory of Bobby Cahill, Visionary Leader, Good Husband, and Loyal Friend." Tony even told Bobby's widow that he would personally make sure the rat who shot him never again saw the light of day, because it certainly must have been some sort of mistake. There was no way Bobby Cahill could have been doing anything wrong.

The day after the funeral, Tony ascended to the director's job, and within three days, most of anything Cahill had in the office was in the trash or in storage at the city shops. Tony's pride and joy was a large, signed mural hanging behind his desk showing the picturesque fourth hole at Riverbend Municipal. It was the site of his first hole-in-one—in fact, the first hole-in-one ever recorded at the golf course. A plaque commemorating the achievement remained on a small mound behind the green. Every time Tony played the course, he made sure to look at the plaque. If he ever saw any tarnish on it, whoever he decided was responsible was immediately transferred from the cushy golf course job to either a garbage truck or the sewer crew. Rarely was the plaque not as shiny as a new half dollar.

Everyone in the City League teed off between 4:30 and 5:15, sometimes 5:30 if there was a bigger turnout than usual. Tony was always in the leadoff group, making sure he was the first in the clubhouse so he could keep a tradition of always buying everyone's first drink, although it was well-known Tony Gallo hadn't paid his tab at the nineteenth hole for decades.

All the golfers took carts, some of them personalized. Tony's cart was painted fire engine red and had headlights, canopy lights, and a working horn that sounded like a siren. Tony loved to drive up the 18th fairway with the canopy lights spinning and the siren wailing. Everyone on the clubhouse patio pretended to love it too.

Tony always teed off first, expecting most of the following golfers to form a fawning gallery. Despite his immense girth, Tony was a deceptively good golfer. He had a wickedly fast, abbreviated backswing that somehow allowed him to put the ball a long way down the middle of most fairways. His strength was his touch around the greens. For a large man, he had amazingly soft hands and an uncanny ability to make putts when he needed them most. It probably didn't hurt that he had each green rolled and manicured to his precise specifications.

"You want to tee off first, Davey?" Tony asked.

Greene knew it was just Tony being deceptively courteous. The right answer, the one he gave was, "No, Tony. It would be bad luck for someone else to take the honors."

"Thanks, Davey," Tony said. "I'll see if I can lead the way." Tony took his blindingly fast swing and put the ball dead center, about a hundred and twenty yards from a pin he had placed himself that morning. The small gallery clapped and whistled. "I got lucky that time. I hope I hit a few more like that today."

For the first four holes, Tony kept up a pleasant banter about the weather, their families, the upcoming meeting at Saratoga Race Course, everything but what Greene figured he really wanted to talk about. The fifth hole was a long, uphill par five at the highest point on the course. From the green, after they had finished the hole, Tony looked back at the valley of Riverbend. "Look at that, Davey," he said, "That's gotta be the prettiest valley in all of New York State." He turned to Greene and gave him a very serious look. "This is a town that can be something great again. It's got everything. Everything except someone to take the place of Wortham. What were we thinking, putting all our eggs in the basket of a broom company." He looked away and laughed. "I guess nobody thought the demand for brooms would ever die. Vacuum cleaners. Goddamn vacuum cleaners killed a whole town. It would be funny as hell if I wasn't staring at the shell of a great city."

Greene said nothing in response. He lived in Riverbend all his life, more outsider than insider, but he still felt most of the same things Tony did.

"You know what it was like watching your town die? We did everything we could once Wortham went downhill. All we wound up with were miserable sweatshops turning out plastic garbage that ain't hardly as good as all that Japanese crap in the five and dime. We used to have a lot of business people and people who worked for the state down in Albany who wanted to live in Riverbend. Now we got a bunch of people who maybe finished the eighth grade and don't speak English who are happy to work for $1.75 an hour. That don't make a town. That makes a rathole. We gotta do something to change that. You, me, all the people who still care about Riverbend."

Greene slumped his shoulders. "What can we do, Tony? Throw out all the people we don't want? Attract some first-rate company? Nobody wants to move to Riverbend. We made every mistake a town can make. And the price of living in Riverbend is going up every year. We charge more in taxes than you pay in midtown Manhattan. Maybe the only reason we live here is that we don't have a better option."

Tony looked like he was going to bark at Greene, but when he finally spoke, it was with a subdued tone. "We're going to put Riverbend back on the map, Davey," Tony said. "You and me and a kid named Mingo."

"What are you talking about, Tony?" Greene asked.

"I'm talking about bowling, that's what I'm talking about. Bowling against the best player in the world. Bowling against him and beating him."

"I still don't get what you're talking about Tony. Who's going to bowl against who?"

"Marcus Aurelius Pandolfo, also known as Mingo, is going to bowl against P. G. Peckham, the guy who put bowling on the map. Right here at Riverbend Alleys."

Greene tilted his head and looked at Tony. "A bowling match is going to save Riverbend? Tony, that's gotta be a stretch even for you."

Tony shook his head at Greene the same way a parent does to a child. "It ain't the bowling match itself. It's exactly what I said before. We're going to make this the party of the decade. And it ain't gonna be just for Riverbend. No, we're gonna have everybody who ever owed me a favor from Brooklyn to Buffalo at this thing. We're not gonna just have a bowling match. We're gonna have an event that shows everyone Riverbend is still where winners live. We're gonna get money and commitments and everything we need to turn the tide in our favor."

"Tony," Greene said, "you need to lay it out straight for me. Right now, it's clear as mud."

"C'mon over to the cart, Davey," Tony said, "and I'll show you exactly what I mean."

It was about a forty-yard walk to where they had left the cart, and Tony covered the ground like an Olympic sprinter. By the time Greene got there, Tony was already unraveling a large document.

"This is it, Davey," he said. "This is what is going to save Riverbend."

Greene looked at the drawing. "It looks like a shopping center."

"That's exactly what it is," Tony said. "It's a mall. An indoor shopping mall. Think of it. You never have to worry about the weather while you are shopping. It can be ten degrees and snowing outside, and you shop in warm comfort."

"I know what a mall is Tony," Greene said. "How does this save Riverbend?"

"That's the beauty. It's where it is that makes the difference. That whole dilapidated downtown gets razed and replaced with new stores. It will be like an injection of adrenaline into Riverbend. People and businesses will move back in. Good people. People with money. They'll bring their fresh-faced kids with them and send them to Riverbend schools. Think of what that will do. More money for education means newer and better schools. Better kids will make the Sweepers teams the envy of the whole league. It will just keep snowballing. The developers will come in and get rid of the low-class housing in the east end and build new houses for the new middle class. They'll build offices for people to work in and supermarkets to shop in and movie theaters to go to on a Friday night. It just goes on and on. Can't you just see it, Davey? You'll be mayor of the most envied city on the east coast."

Greene looked at the sketches. He thought, *He's nuts. Tony has finally cracked.* Instead, he said, "Well, maybe it would be a shot in the arm. But who is going to pay for this? Who is going to pay to change all the roads? What about all the businesses who are already down there? What do we do with them?"

"Jeez, Davey, have some vision here." Greene could see Tony getting annoyed. "Lemme ask you this. You got a better idea?"

"No, Tony," Greene said, "I don't have a better idea. I guess maybe a change that big is just going to take me some time to absorb."

Tony did his best to sound sympathetic. "Of course. It is a lot of change. But I know it can work. It's the future, Davey. And we get to be the architects. Don't worry about the businesses. The first thing we do is start condemning the buildings that were probably going to fall down in a few years anyway. The ones we can't condemn, we use our city powers to buy, at fair market value of course. Don't kid yourself, Davey. When we show up, they will ask to sign before we even get done explaining the whole thing to them. The only guy who is going to make noise is Buddy Frank. 'Course his clothing store, Storman's, is the only one making money down there. That's where you can help out, Davey."

"Me? Why me?"

"Because you and Buddy Frank are, you know, connected."

"Connected?" Greene asked.

"Yeah," Tony said. "Like on Saturdays. You both go to the same church."

"You mean synagogue? And you think that connects us? Is everyone who shows up at Most Precious Blood on Sunday your good friend? Never mind...dumb question."

Tony smiled. "Well, sure. I think if Frank listens to anyone, it would be you. You're both Jewish. That's like being family, ain't it?

93

Plus, you're the mayor. He's gotta know if anyone would give it to him straight, it would be you."

Greene seethed at the suggestion being Jewish was somehow like being members of the same secret cult. But now wasn't the time to argue with Tony. He also wondered why this was the first time he was hearing about plans to change the whole city. That damn Tony would go too far one of these days, and when he did, David Greene and Elliot Levine would be there to watch him get what he deserved.

"I need to understand this a lot better before I talk with anyone, Tony," Greene said. "I gotta internalize this, you know what I mean?"

"Of course, Davey." Tony smiled. "You and me, we're gonna have statues in the center of the mall. Gallo and Greene. Visionaries of Riverbend. Whatever you need, let me know. We're partners now, Davey. Partners in the restoration of Riverbend. Don't it sound grand?"

"Yeah, Tony. It sounds spectacular." Greene momentarily hoped someone would hit him in the head with a golf ball so he could be laid up until the whole shopping mall mess was over.

"Hey, Davey," Tony said. "You won that hole. Your honors. Show us the way. Show us the way home."

CHAPTER 20

Sundays in Riverbend were quiet. Fazzone's drug store was open for a couple of hours in the morning so people could have coffee after church, but that was pretty much the only place that unlocked its doors during the day. Of course, if you knew the right password, some of the locked doors at the many taverns in town might open up for a beer and a shot to prepare for one of Father Monticello's endless homilies.

Vinnie's family and mine faithfully attended the eleven o'clock mass at Most Precious Blood, and after church, our parents allowed us to walk home together. Even though it was only about a fifteen-minute walk from the church, Vinnie and I usually managed to drag it out for about an hour. It was fine as long as we weren't late for Sunday dinner at two. At our houses, Sunday dinner was at least as important as going to church on Sunday.

Often, we would sit on the rocks along the banks of Ohneka Creek. The creek ran from the high area near the golf course all the way through town to the Mohawk River. Years earlier, factories dumped their waste into the creek, sometimes causing it to change colors. We were pretty sure the creek was devoid of any aquatic life by the time it emptied into the river.

The last Sunday in July was hot and humid, what people called muggy. The sun was a hazy, shimmering ball, radiating the heavy air with a few more degrees every hour. Vinnie and I were throwing pebbles into the creek, mesmerized by the water tumbling by.

I spoke first. "What do you think happened to Albert?"

Vinnie replied, "I don't know. My grandma says people who drink too much are being controlled by the devil. Of course, she thinks anyone who does anything wrong is being controlled by the devil."

"He looks so sad all the time," I said. "Like he doesn't care what happens to him. But I think deep down he is a pretty nice man. I think he just needs something to care about."

"Maybe we can get him a dog," Vinnie said.

"I don't mean like that. I mean something that makes you want to be more than a pin boy."

We sat there silently for a while, throwing more pebbles into the water. I broke the silence again. "I know you can go to hell for marrying a Protestant, but what if you just go to the movies with one?"

"What movie would you see?" Vinnie asked.

"What difference does that make? Just a movie. Like maybe a matinee. A double feature. With a cartoon."

Vinnie mused a bit. "That's a tough one. Would you actually go into their house to pick up the girl? 'Cause I think that might be the same as going into their church, and I know you can go to hell for that."

"I could stand on the porch and wait. If they invited me in, I could tell them I was allergic to carpet or something."

Vinnie shook his head. "No, you can't say that. There is carpet everywhere. You'd have to fake an allergic reaction every time you went anywhere. I think if you say three Hail Mary's and make an Act of Contrition, you can go into the house, cause I gotta think even God would have to walk into a Protestant's house if the girl's parents invited him in. As long as you say the prayers, I think you can turn it into a venial sin." Vinnie paused a moment. "I think it's gotta be okay to go into the movies. I mean, there's already gonna be Protestants in the theater, and it ain't a sin to sit in the same movie theater with 'em."

"What if I held her hand?" I asked.

Vinnie was direct. "That's not a gray area, I don't think. I think maybe you could accidentally touch each other's hands, like if you were both reaching into the bag of popcorn at the same time or something, but if you did it on purpose, that would be a sin."

Vinnie's look brightened. "Hey, I know what you can do. You can go to the Bijou on a Saturday afternoon. That's right across from Most Precious Blood. Confessions start at four o'clock. You hold hands, get out of the theater, tell her you gotta drop something off inside and go do a confession. As long as you don't get hit by a car crossing the street, you're back in heaven."

"Yeah, that sounds like it could work. But how are we going to get Saturday afternoon off? I mean, they could cover for one of us, but not two, I don't think," I said.

Vinnie turned to me. "We? What do you mean we? Wait a minute. You're not thinking of going to the movies with Charlie Horse, are you?"

"Why not? Don't you think she would go with me?"

Vinnie laughed. "G and Charlie Horse. Wait until I tell Borneo."

I frowned at him. "You better not say anything. I don't want her to know about it until I am sure she will say yes."

"Oh, she'll say yes all right. Nobody can resist Italian charm. C'mon, G, let's get going. I'm getting hungry. We're having *mostacioli calabrese* and chicken today. I don't want to be late 'cause my big brothers can each eat a pound of pasta and a hen on their own. They have no family loyalty when it comes to eating."

We took a shortcut through a delivery alley between some of the abandoned factories. Suddenly, Vinnie stopped. "You hear that, G?"

"Hear what? I didn't hear anything."

"Stay quiet a minute. There, did you hear that right there? It sounded like voices and banging."

Vinnie was right. Something was going on in one of the side alleys ahead. "I hear it now. It's coming from up there."

Both of us took off running, and as we got closer to the alley, we could hear voices getting louder. We stopped short of the alley opening and cautiously peered around the corner.

Vinnie looked at me and said in the faintest of whispers, "Omigod, it's Danny."

Sure enough, the same three greasers who got thrown out of the bowling alley that one night had backed Danny up against the wall at the end of the alley. Danny held the lid of a garbage can in his hand, fending off the boys who were trying to jab at him with short pieces of wood. They were taking their time, tormenting Danny, who had a look of real terror on his face.

"What are we gonna do?" Vinnie asked.

"Well, we gotta help Danny ourselves," I said. "There's no way we can run and get some help. By the time we get back, those guys will have already hurt him."

"Yeah, but we're not big enough to take those guys on," Vinnie said. "If we run down the alley, they'll kill us too." Vinnie paused a moment. "I got an idea. First, let's see if the door to this building is locked. If you can get inside, up to the second floor, maybe you can distract them for a few minutes. That should be all I need."

"You want me to distract them? What are you going to be doing in the meantime?" I asked.

"Don't worry about me. You just get up there and distract them. I'll take care of the rest. Let's try the door."

The door was locked but had been broken off its bottom hinge just enough for a boy my size to squeeze through.

"Get going, G. And don't worry. The cavalry's coming."

I had no doubt. I would have trusted Vinnie to the ends of the earth. He took off on the dead run, and I slipped through the small opening. It was dusty inside, and the air smelled rank, almost dead. I located the stairs and bounded up to the second floor. I went to the wall that overlooked the alley and saw the boys had closed in a little on Danny. Danny was as strong as a horse, but even he would have been no match for the three toughs. Plus, given Danny's disability, he probably would have been too afraid to think clearly.

One of the boys, the one who had been incapacitated by the bowling ball, said to Danny, "You aren't so tough when you don't have the other losers around to protect you, are you, retard?"

Danny just looked at him, too petrified to even speak. His lip was quivering, and he looked like he was about to cry.

I looked around the factory floor. There was plenty of debris, even some boxes of hardware that must have been left over from the days when the plant was operating. I found a small box of steel washers and carried it over to the window. Some of the glass had been broken by kids who thought it was fun to throw rocks at windows, so there were plenty of openings for me. I took the washer like I was throwing a frisbee and launched it out one of the openings, making sure I stayed far enough back so they couldn't see me if they looked up.

It hit one of them on the back, not very hard, but hard enough to distract him. "What the hell was that?" he said.

"What was what?" his partners asked him.

"Something hit me. Something hard." He looked down and saw the washer on the ground. He bent over to pick it up and said, "It was this. A washer hit me."

His friends started laughing. "Right. It's raining washers now. It probably just came loose from the building. C'mon, we need to take care of the retard."

They turned back to Danny, and I threw a second washer, hitting one of the other boys. "Hey," he said, "what are you doing? Don't throw that washer at me."

"I didn't throw anything," the first boy said.

"Then who hit me with that washer?"

"I don't know, but maybe we ought to finish what we started here."

Once again, they turned toward Danny, and once again, I launched a washer. This time one of the boys looked up immediately and caught a glimpse of me. "Up there," he shouted. "That's where they're coming from. Someone is up there throwing them at us."

The biggest boy said, "You guys stay here and watch the retard. I'll take care of the wise guy in the building."

He left the alley, looking for an entrance to get inside. He saw the door I had used, but quickly realized he couldn't squeeze through the same opening. He started kicking at it with his heavy boot, slowly enlarging the opening. It took him a few minutes, but he finally got into the factory.

"You're dead, kid, wherever you are," he yelled. "I'm going to break every bone in your body when I get my hands on you."

He looked for the way upstairs, and when he located the staircase, I could hear him clomping up one stair at a time. I moved to one of the interior walls, hoping that by being in the shadows he would initially miss me. I also figured he would look first at the windows. He got to the top of the stairs and, as expected, walked over to the window side. I took one of my washers and threw it into the corner farthest from the stairs.

"Now I got you, kid," he said.

When he started walking toward the corner, I took off for the stairs. He turned and saw me and began to run toward me, but I hit the staircase first and headed directly for the open door. I slid out easily and turned toward the side alley, hoping I could distract the other two boys. Unfortunately, one of them had moved to the top of the alley and, just as I was ready to run by, jumped out and grabbed me.

"Let me go, you big dufus," I yelled, but he was far too strong for me. He carried me to the end of the alley and threw me at Danny.

I looked at Danny and said, "Don't worry. Vinnie will be back with help. Just hang on, Danny. We're going to be all right."

Danny just gave me a frozen look.

By that time, the boy who had chased me in the factory made it outside and joined the others in the alley.

"You, you're the other big mouth pin boy. We're gonna teach you a lesson you won't forget. You won't be setting pins anymore, unless they have an alley in the hospital." They all laughed.

I looked at them and said, "Well, maybe you should think about that a minute. Maybe those guys behind you might have a different opinion."

"Kid, that's the oldest trick in the book. If you think we're falling for that while you and the retard try to make a run for it, maybe you're retarded too."

"Okay," I said, "have it your way. But I never tell a lie. Don't say I didn't warn you."

The three boys started howling with laughter. "He don't give up, does he," the biggest one said.

A voice came from behind them. "And why should he? After all, like G said, he don't ever tell a lie."

All of a sudden the boys stopped laughing and turned around. At the end of the alley were the three Antonioni brothers with Vinnie in front of them grinning. Standing shoulder to shoulder, they were almost wide enough to block the entire alley opening.

"We don't have no beef with you guys," one said.

The oldest brother, named Pietro after his father, but called Pepe by everyone, said, "As it turns out you do. You see, we got a thing about losers who pick on our family and friends, 'cause where we come from, there ain't nothing more important than family and friends. That would make you guys our problem."

"We were just having fun. We weren't gonna hurt nobody."

"That's good," Pepe said. "'Cause if you had, there wouldn't have been enough of you left in this alley to put in a shoebox. And you see, that not only goes for now, but it goes for the rest of time." He motioned at me. "C'mere, little G. And bring Danny with you."

I tugged at Danny's sleeve, but he was frozen in place. "C'mon, Danny. It's okay. Everything is okay now."

He relaxed a little, put down the garbage can lid, and walked with me toward the Antonioni brothers.

The third Antonioni brother, Mikey, who was also slightly the biggest of the three, said, "Vinnie, G, you take Danny home. Have Ma give him some soup. We'll make sure these guys don't cause any more trouble. We'll be along in a little bit. We'll give Danny a ride home in the dump truck. I'll bet he'll get a kick out of that."

We started walking home. I said, "Well, you could have cut it a little closer. I figure Danny and I had at least another minute or so to live."

Vinnie laughed. "Don't I always come through, G? You never had a worry."

I laughed too. I turned to Danny. "You okay, Danny?"

He started crying, in big heaving sobs. "I didn't know what to do. I thought they were gonna break my watch. I didn't know what to do."

Vinnie said, "Hey, Danny, you oughta know by now we pin boys take care of each other. As long as me and G are around, we'll all watch out for each other."

We went to Vinnie's house where his mother gave Danny some soup and Italian bread with olive oil and salt. A short time later the Antonioni brothers came home, looking slightly sweaty, but not the slightest bit disheveled.

"Thanks a lot, you guys," I said. "I was never so happy to see anyone in my life."

Pepe said, "I meant what I said, G. You take care of your family and friends. No matter what. Even if sometimes they get on your nerves. When everything else is said and done, they're the ones who matter most."

"What happened to those guys in the alley?" I asked.

The middle brother, Louie, said, "Well, let's just say they went from greasers to grease spots. I don't think they'll be giving anyone any trouble for a while."

Almost in unison, the three Antonioni brothers, yelled, "Hey, Ma, is it time to eat yet? We're starved."

Maria Antonioni walked out of the kitchen with a sauce covered wooden spoon in her hand. "The next one who tries to rush my dinner won't get any zabaglione for dessert. Now go wash up. You boys aren't going to eat at my table with dirty hands and faces. Hurry up now."

I laughed out loud. "I guess we all know who is really the toughest Antonioni."

The three hulking brothers said, "You got that right, G."

Maria Antonioni smiled. "I gotta go cook," and she walked back into the kitchen.

CHAPTER 21

Albert sat on the bank of the Mohawk, back resting against a tree. As usual, he had a paper bag with a quart of beer hidden inside. He took a long pull and stared out at the river. Borneo came out of the bowling alley and stood next to Albert.

"River always looks calm, doesn't it?" Borneo said, "But the surface fools you. Underneath that river is full of currents and eddies. It's like a whole different world under the water. Sort of like people, don't you think?"

"I don't know much about people," Albert said.

Borneo just nodded. "Everyone's got a story, Albert," Borneo said. "What's yours? What's under your surface?"

"I got nothing to talk about, Borneo. It was all a long time ago anyway. I just want to set pins, get enough money for beer, and hope I find some place warm to sleep at night."

Borneo threw some stones in the river. "River is interesting. Sometimes it's hard, like when you try to skip a stone. It bounces across the river. Sometimes it's soft and just swallows your stone." Borneo looked down at Albert. "You don't have to be hard all the time, Albert. Sometimes it's good to talk about things. Get some weight off your shoulders."

Albert started talking. "It was June 2, 1944. Three days to go. Three days until we were supposed to storm the beach in Normandy. It was four days until my eighteenth birthday. I figured I would never see it." Albert picked at his fingernails and took another pull on his bottle.

"We were in a place called Portsmouth, England. Coldest, wettest place I'd ever been to. Everyone in the barracks was jittery. Some of the men played cards, some threw dice, some just sat on their cots and smoked cigarettes. I thought about my mother back in Riverbend. She had tossed my father out when I was eight. I guess she finally couldn't take him drinking away his paycheck every week. I maybe saw him once or twice after that, wandering through town. I couldn't be sure though. Didn't look nothing like the man who taught me how to throw a baseball and ride a bike." Albert paused and looked down at the ground.

"I didn't always look like this. When I was sixteen, I was tall and I had plenty of muscles. Pretty much looked like a man. Back then—it was 1943—Riverbend was a workingman's town. Seemed like there was a tavern about on every corner. Most of them were full most nights. Bet you didn't know back then, Riverbend had more bars than any town its size in the whole state. It seemed like that's what there was to do in Riverbend. It wasn't hard to convince the bartenders I was old enough, but I swore I wasn't going to be a drunk like my father. Just have one once in a while to relax. You know." He took another swig and started talking again.

"The bars closed at two just like now, although most places just locked the door and let everyone already inside keep drinking. One night, I was in the bar, drinking VO and Vichy until four in the morning. First time I was really drunk. They let me out the door, and I started stumbling home. I looked up, and there he was, walking toward me. Tony Gallo, Jr. He was a jerk, just like his father. Thought he owned the town and everyone in it. He said something to me, and I slugged him. Hard. Left him lying on the curb. Next morning, the cops came for me. I sat in jail three days before they got around to taking me to court. I figured I'd get probation or something, but you didn't mess with the Gallos. My lawyer laid it out for me. Tony Gallo wanted to see me sent upstate, and the district attorney wasn't going to get in the way. But it turns out, the judge was no fan of Tony Gallo, and he let my lawyer know if I was willing to join the military, he'd let me off. So I joined the army.

"In April 1943, I got sent to Fort Wolters in Texas to be trained as an infantryman. I hadn't been out of Riverbend unless you count Albany. Ever been to Texas? Couldn't figure out why anyone would want to live there unless they had no choice like me. I was trained until September, and then they sent me to the First Infantry Division in Sicily. Called us the Big Red One. I thought it was funny that I might have to kill my own relatives. My last name is Ferraro, from Paterno in case you didn't know. By November, we were moved to England. We weren't told much, but we knew something big was up. Eventually, we figured out that we were going across the channel to Normandy. We trained hard for months. The commanders kept telling us how important we were gonna be to winning the war. Pumpin' us up, trying to get us not to think about dyin'." He stopped again.

"You were a soldier, Borneo. Only way to not think about dyin' is to fog your brain up with something. Dyin' was all I could think of, and I didn't sign up to die. I just wanted to get away from Tony Gallo."

Borneo remembered Vietnam. Seemed like half his unit was doing heroin. Yeah, that kept you from thinking about dying.

"I'd managed to keep a fifth of scotch in my footlocker. I figured if I didn't have a drink right then, that bottle might just go to waste. Just a drink. Something to steady my nerves, make me stop thinking about getting shot. I put the bottle under my coat and went outside to just take a swig." One more pull from the bottle in the bag and the quart was finished. Albert wasn't.

"I woke up about four hours later in the brig. I remember my left eye was closed, and my head felt like someone was pounding from the inside trying to get out. An MP walked by. I asked him, 'What happened? What am I doing here?' He didn't say nothin'. 'C'mon,' I said, 'I'm shipping out of here in three days. I need to get back to my unit.' 'You won't be going anywhere, soldier,' said the MP. 'Your tour of duty ended when the sergeant died.' 'Died? What are you talking about, died?' I said. I didn't remember a thing.

"I had a trial. Seems that one of the sergeants found me behind the barracks. By that time, I had finished the bottle and was dozing off. He grabbed the bottle, and I guess he punched me in the eye. I was startled, like I was being attacked by the Nazis, I guess, and all I could think of was to hit him back. They said I hit him hard enough to crack his skull. Said I hit him a bunch of times. Bein' drunk ain't no defense, but I guess that and the fact the sergeant hit me first was enough that they only convicted me of manslaughter. I got a dishonorable discharge and was shipped to the military penitentiary at Leavenworth. Ten years, they gave me. I served most of it. I thought a lot in prison. I didn't think about beating the sergeant. I still couldn't remember anything about that. I thought about not landing on Omaha beach. I thought about all the people in my unit who died as heroes. I thought, I should have been there. I should have died a hero too. Not the drunken son of a drunk." He looked up at Borneo.

"You know how many guys from the First Infantry were killed or wounded? 1,638. And I wasn't one of them. I made my way back to Riverbend. By then, my ma had died. I don't know if it was from shame or just years of working too hard to see I didn't grow up like my father. I tried to get a job. Wasn't easy. Everyone knew who I was, what I had done. I did odd jobs, mostly when people felt sorry for me. So I just started drinking more. Trying to forget." Albert looked out at the river.

"You know what, Borneo. You don't forget. No matter how much alcohol you drink. It always comes back." And with that, Albert stood up, took a step forward, and jumped in the river.

CHAPTER 22

I had just come out to get Borneo and Albert. Borneo looked back and saw me and yelled, "Albert's in the river. Get help, G."

Who was I going to get? Danny? Frank? Yakky? I didn't think they would be much help, and it was Vinnie's day off, so I wouldn't be able to count on him. I could see Borneo bent over, looking at the river, looking for Albert.

I turned and ran inside yelling, "Albert's fallen in the river. We have to save him!"

Frank immediately picked up the phone and dialed someone. Yakky ran outside. I ran to the cleaning closet. I grabbed a couple of the empty banana oil cans. I figured they were big enough to float and grab onto. There was a long extension cord hanging on a nail on the wall. I grabbed it and slung it across my shoulder. Finally, I grabbed a lane mop. The handle was pretty long, and I thought we could pull him in if he got close enough to grab hold of it.

I ran back out. Yakky turned to me. "Where's Borneo?"

"He was standing there when I went inside," I said.

"He must have jumped in after him," Yakky said.

"But he can't swim. Borneo can't swim. He told me himself."

"I don't see them," said Yakky. "Maybe the current is moving them down the river."

We started running along the bank, scanning the river. "I see Borneo," I said.

Borneo was splashing in the water, yelling for help and desperately trying to stay afloat.

"He's too far away for the pole," I said.

"Wait," said Yakky, "it's Albert. He's swimming toward Borneo."

Borneo disappeared under the water just before Albert got to him. We could see Albert dive under after him. We watched the river for a minute, and then Albert exploded to the surface with a firm hold on Borneo. Albert was struggling to hold Borneo and fight the current.

"We need help," yelled Albert.

I pulled the extension cord off and looped one of the ends through the handles on both of the empty banana oil cans and tied a knot. I swung the cans over my head and let them fly just above where Albert was trying to hold Borneo. They floated down but the cans were short of where Albert could grab them.

"A little farther," said Albert, "just a little farther."

I hauled the cans in and spun them over my head, flinging them as far as I possibly could.

They came close enough for Albert to grab on. "Now pull us in," Albert yelled.

"C'mon, Yakky," I said, "help me pull."

We got them into shore, and Albert pulled Borneo out of the water. He wasn't moving.

"We've got to do something," I said.

"Maybe those guys can help," Yakky said, motioning at two firemen rushing toward us.

"Step aside, boys," one of the men said, "we'll take it from here."

The firemen started working on him, and all of a sudden, he started coughing and spitting up water.

"Is he going to be okay?" I asked.

"Yeah," said the fireman. "He'll be fine. We're going to take him to Most Precious Blood Hospital to have him checked out."

They put Borneo on a gurney and took him to the hospital.

I looked at Albert. "What happened?"

"I... I fell in, I guess. Borneo must have come in after me," Albert said. "I need to see if he is okay. I'm going to the hospital."

Albert walked to the hospital and stayed in the waiting room for about an hour. A nurse came by to tell him it was all right to visit his friend.

"Thanks for saving me," Albert said.

"I think you may have that the other way around," Borneo replied. "I just jumped in after you. I forgot for a moment I can't swim."

"Why did you do it? Why didn't you just let the river take me?"

Borneo looked right at Albert. "Dunno. I guess it's because we're brothers. Because we both got broken by wars that we didn't want to fight in. Because we're both wasting whatever little talent we might have setting pins in a bowling alley."

He coughed a little.

"The thought that went through my head was that I had seen all the dying because of war I was willing to take. I'm done letting that war control my life. You need to be done with it too, Albert. Yeah, it was a bad thing you did, but you were a seventeen-year-old kid. Scared, just like we all were. Trying to find a way to stay alive for one more day."

"I don't know, Borneo," said Albert. "I don't know if I can face the world—face myself sober all the time."

"There was a point when I was feeling like the river was grabbing hold of me. When it was pulling me down and I was never going to come back. And then I felt a hand grab me. And I knew two things. I wanted to live. I wanted to live worse than anything. And I wasn't going to hide anymore. I was going to find all the scared and broken soldiers who came home from wars and couldn't figure out how to be part of the regular world and I was going to tell them they weren't alone. They didn't have to act like no one understood what they were going through.

"We'd form a group, a council. We'd talk with other people who knew what we saw, what we went through. It didn't matter if anyone else cared. We would care. We would care for each other. At that moment, I knew I wanted to live more than anything." He grabbed Albert's hand. "Promise me you'll help me. Promise me you'll be part of it."

Albert started crying. "Sure, Borneo," he said. "I'll help you. I'm just as tired of hiding in a bottle. I'm tired of everyone making fun of me. I'm tired of thinking that I'm so worthless it didn't matter if I was alive or dead. I'll do whatever you want me to."

CHAPTER 23

Tony Sharp was asleep on his stool when Tony Gallo walked in. He boomed at him, "Tony Sharp, report for duty." Tony Sharp jumped to his feet and did his best to come to attention. Tony Gallo started laughing.

"Geez, Tony, you don't have to treat me like I'm General MacArthur or something. It's just regular old Tony Gallo. How's it going, Tony? Business a little slow today?"

Tony Sharp stammered out, "It's always a little slow in the afternoons, Mr. Gallo."

Gallo walked over and slapped him heartily on the back. "Hey, we've known each other a long time. Just call me Tony."

"Sure, Mr. Gallo. I mean, Tony."

"Is Paulie around? I need to talk with him."

"He's in the back lookin' at the Telly." The Telly referred to the *Morning Telegraph*, the broadsheet newspaper that contained information on race horses. "Saratoga opening day is tomorrow, and Paulie figures business will be booming. He's gettin' ready."

It was a widely known secret that even though race tracks had long since abandoned bookmakers in favor of pari-mutuel machines, people still needed to make bets on days when they couldn't make it to the track. There were public phones at the track, but they were all turned off once the races started, and it was inconceivable in 1968 to ever think rotary dial telephones would someday be replaced by portable phones the size of a deck of cards. It would also be a few years before states figured out they could replace one more aspect of the bookmaking profession with their own off track betting parlors, so whether you wanted to bet some big race or your birthday in the daily double, the local bookmaker was pretty much the only option. The phones at Paulie DiMeo's place were never turned off.

The opening of Saratoga Race Course in August was an epic event in that part of the state. All of racing's royal families made the pilgrimage to the meet, landing at the historic and extravagant Gideon Putnam Hotel, while casual race fans from New York City to Buffalo filled up every hotel from Albany to Glens Falls.

Paulie DiMeo figured August was good for about half his annual income. All he had to watch out for was any wise guy trying to break the bookmakers with a longshot steamer. Even though Paulie had been banned from Saratoga as a convicted bookmaker, he still fancied himself a better judge of horses than 99 percent of the people placing bets with him. He figured this gave him an edge when deciding how much action to take himself and how much to lay off with some of his competitors. "They say you can't beat the races," Paulie mused. "Turns out you just have to be on the right side of the bet."

The bell from the front—two short rings and a long one— let Paulie know he had a friendly visitor waiting. Paulie emerged through the meat locker door, and Tony Gallo greeted him with the traditional hug and kiss, practically enveloping the far smaller man. Paulie thought, *This* is not *my lucky day.*

"Paulie, *paisan*," Tony said. "How's every little thing? Business good?"

"Couldn't be better, my friend," Paulie said. "It's gonna be a busy month for me. They say it's gonna be a record meet at the Spa."

"Yeah, I'll be there for the Riverbend Stakes. They asked me to hand out the trophy this year."

Paulie wasn't going to wait for Tony to work up to whatever was on his mind. "How 'bout we go in the back, Tony, maybe have some espresso and sambuca."

"Lead the way," Gallo said, and they disappeared through the heavy metal door, leaving Tony Sharp to wipe the accumulated nervous sweat from his face.

Paulie started brewing the coffee. Tony lit a DiNobili and started talking. "How long we known each other, Paulie?"

"Since we were kids," he said. "You know that."

"And in all that time, haven't I taken care of you? You got a bunch of other bookmakers get busted twice a year, but you only been busted that once when I was out of town."

"You know I appreciate it," Paulie said. He thought a moment and added, "It's been a good friendship for both of us."

"That's what friendship's all about, Paulie. You watch my back, I watch yours. Let me get right to the point. You know about the downtown mall, right?"

"Yeah, I heard some things," he said.

"I want you in on it," Tony said. "Naturally, you'd have to be a silent partner until we got all the money in place."

"Naturally." Paulie hoped that didn't sound too harsh. "How much you figurin' on involving me?"

"I don't have an exact number right this minute. I been talking to the state guys. They have a bunch of money for something they're calling urban renewal. We'll get new roads, a new bridge from the South Side into downtown. It'll be like a brand spankin' new city. And that mall. We're gonna have everything from Macy's to Tiffany's. Not a bunch of cheesy five-and-dime-type stores. Upscale shops that are gonna serve an upscale city. A first-rate movie theater that'll put the Bijou to shame. We'll drive out the riff raff, do urban renewal from the east end to the west side and up Slav Hill. New houses, new factories making first-rate American stuff, not a bunch of cheap plastic crap. People with money are gonna be pushin' each other aside just to live in the greatest little city in New York—Riverbend. The state guys said if we're one of the cities picked, they'll put up most of the money, but, ya know, we gotta show some good faith cash to make up the difference. I'm not gonna lie to you. Riverbend is broke. Any money is gonna have to come from the people who still got some cash available. 'Course, they're all gonna make ten times whatever they put in. We got some time before we have to send the state any official paperwork, but it turns out, I got an immediate need."

Paulie handed Tony his demitasse and a bottle of sambuca. "You gotta grease some palms?" Paulie asked.

Tony poured about half of the coffee in the demitasse into the saucer. He filled up the cup with the sambuca. He took a large sip. "That's good espresso, Paulie. Damn good espresso." He took a few puffs on his cigar and then continued. "Not exactly. I need you to handle the action on the match between Mingo and P. G. Peckham."

"Back up a minute. What match? What action? What are you talkin' about?"

"You know Mingo, right?"

"I heard of him. Some hotshot bowler, ain't he?"

"Everybody says he's the best. Could maybe go pro someday."

"And he's bowling against this…who'd you say his name was?"

"Peckham," Tony said. "P. G. Peckham. Best pro bowler in the country."

Paulie was working hard at staying calm. The only thing he knew for sure about Tony's schemes was that Tony never came out on the short end. "Lay it out for me, Tony. What exactly are we talking about?"

"Peckham does this barnstorming thing where he goes around to different towns and bowls against the best local talent. Hasn't lost in three years. He usually gets some money just for showing up, but he makes his real money betting on himself. Lately, that hasn't been so lucrative. Who the hell bets when you're just tossing good money away?"

"You'd be surprised," Paulie said.

"Well, I got a different plan. Mingo is gonna beat Peckham."

"You sure of that?" Paulie asked.

"I'm positive," Tony said. He looked hard at Paulie. "Just let me worry about the bowling match."

"So where exactly do I come in?"

"You're booking the bets. And you're making Mingo a 10-1 underdog."

"Listen, Tony. You might know a lot about most things, but you don't know too much about booking."

"I only play when I know I'm gonna win, Paulie."

Paulie looked at him with a sideways glance. "Who's gonna bet on Peckham at those odds? Everyone knows you bet a little to win a lot, and the only way to do that is to bet on Mingo. If all the action's on Mingo, I'll take a bath when he wins."

Tony pondered for a moment. "Yeah, you're right. It ain't my business. I'll leave it to you to figure it out." Tony paused again. "Peckham is gonna get ten grand just for losing."

"Where you comin' up with the ten large?" Paulie thought he might know the answer.

"Peckham is betting on Mingo. I know that, Peckham and his manager know that, and now you know that. You're paying off the bet. Peckham walks out of here with ten thousand clams, the state people I'm gonna invite for the day see why Riverbend is the city they want to pick for urban renewal, and we'll have our own local celebrity bowler. Look, if you're smart you'll figure out how to make sure more people bet on Peckham than Mingo. It'll all be gravy for you. Mingo is gonna win the match. You're just sort of makin' sure everyone is happy at the end of the night."

"You know what they say about things that look too good to be true, Tony," Paulie said.

"Most of the people who say that don't do all their homework. I got everything figured down to the last detail." Tony gave Paulie a fatherly look. "You know I asked you because I can trust you. I'm gonna make you rich and give you more respectability than you can ever get bookin' horses and payin' off on the number. You're gonna be a businessman. You'll go from bein' a regular crook to bein' a respectable crook like all the other guys who are puttin' up money." Tony laughed at his joke. Paulie didn't. "You'll be Paulie DiMeo, businessman. Pillar of the community and all that. You might even have to learn how to golf." Tony laughed again.

"When's this match gonna happen?" Paulie asked.

"Labor Day. Saratoga's over by then, and all the people who bet in August will be lookin' to get some money back. And get this. We're havin' it at the Riverbend Alleys. That old claptrap is gonna be famous as the place where P. G. Peckham met his match."

Paulie was resigned. "You know you can count on me, Tony."

Tony said, "I never doubted that for a second. Now what do you say you pour me another half cup of that delicious espresso." He held the demitasse up. "*Salud, paisan. Alla prosperità.*"

CHAPTER 24

It was a strange Wednesday. Albert and Borneo almost drowned. Lucky for us, with Saratoga open, fewer people were around to bowl, and Danny, Crackers, Charlie Horse, and I were able to handle the few people who showed up. I said goodbye to everyone and started home, turning right from the bowling alley toward the east end. I noticed it wasn't as hot outside as it was in the bowling alley, and I felt silly for not grabbing a cold soda before leaving. I hadn't gone a block when I noticed a car following me. It was a bright yellow Oldsmobile 88 convertible, with an engine that sounded like someone gargling. I walked a little faster, but the Oldsmobile kept up. I wasn't going to outrun it. I wondered where the Antonioni brothers might be.

It pulled up alongside me. It was Mingo.

"Hey, G," he said, "need a ride home?"

"I'm good," I said. "Nice night for a walk."

"Hop in," he said. "I need to talk with you about something. It's important."

I got in. "Nice car," I said.

"Chicks love it," he said. "Cost me two grand used, but worth every cent. C'mon, we'll take a quick spin around the city."

Mingo turned left up Storie Street and headed into the middle of Slav Hill. The Olds slipped up the hill effortlessly.

"What did you want to talk with me about?" I asked.

"You heard about the match, right," he said. "Me and P. G. Peckham."

"Yeah, Labor Day. Last day I'll be a pin boy before school starts," I said.

"I'm going to win, you know. There's nobody in the world that can beat me at Riverbend Alleys."

"It's always good to be confident," I said. "Was that what was so important to tell me?"

Mingo momentarily looked like a normal human being. "Who am I fooling," he said. "I'm scared to death. You don't know what it's like to have Tony Gallo throwing that meaty arm around you telling you you're going to bowl the best bowler in the world and the whole town will be counting on you. He was trying to be nice, but I could tell there was something more to it. Like it wasn't just supposed to be a friendly match but something bigger. I don't know what."

Mingo had caught me off guard. "You're a pretty good bowler," I said. "If anyone can beat Peckham, you can."

"Maybe," Mingo said.

Mingo gunned the car down Forbes Street and squealed around the corner at Division Street. "I gotta win this match," Mingo said. "You know what it'll mean for me? I can become a pro bowler, make money doing the thing I'm best at. Maybe the only thing I'm really good at. No more working at my old man's supermarket, lifting boxes, sweeping sawdust, stocking shelves. I'll have it all. Money, fame, and a way out of this dying rathole of a town. You understand?"

"Here's the strange thing," Mingo said. "Tony Gallo made it sound like I wouldn't have any problem at all winning. And he's never even seen me bowl. This was the last thing he said to me. You just bowl. It will all work out fine. I know this much. You don't say no to Tony Gallo."

"I don't know much about Tony Gallo, except what you hear around town," I said. "But I've seen you bowl, and we all know why he picked you. He believes you can win." I knew I'd have to go to confession for what I said next. "We all think you're the best, Mingo. Every pin boy at the alley will be rooting for you."

"You think so?" Mingo said. "You really think I can beat him?"

"There's probably five bowlers in the Pro League who can beat him, and you beat them every week. Peckham won't know what hit him," I said.

"Listen, G. I know the pin boys ain't so happy with me. I can be a little tough on you guys," Mingo said.

A little tough, I thought. Like Bruno Sammartino was tough on Gorilla Monsoon.

"I want you to be the foul spotter," Mingo said. "Everybody knows you'll be honest. I need someone who won't be afraid to call a foul on Peckham if he crosses over the line."

"Sure, Mingo," I said. "Better to watch the match from the front than back in the cave."

"Who do you think should set pins?" Mingo asked.

"Borneo definitely. And probably Danny," I said.

"You sure?" Mingo said. "I don't think they like me very much since what happened earlier this summer."

Another trip to the confessional for me. "Nah," I said, "they forgot about that a long time ago. They're the two best pinsetters we got. You know that. They'd be proud to be the pinsetters."

Mingo looked relieved. "I was worried, G," he said. "I thought maybe everyone's personal feelings might make some problems."

Oh well. I might as well make confession worthwhile. "Don't worry about a thing, Mingo. We're going to be rooting for you with all we've got."

"Thanks, G," Mingo said. "I'll square it with Frank. C'mon, I'll drop you home."

CHAPTER 25

Vinnie picked me up in the morning on Friday as usual. I asked him if he had heard about the excitement from Wednesday, and he said Yakky blabbed the whole thing. I told him about my ride with Mingo.

"I can't believe you got in the car with him," Vinnie said. "You're lucky to be alive. You should have seen him last night. He was screaming and yelling and being his regular Mingo self."

"He's really not that bad," I said. "I think deep down he's almost a regular human being. I think mostly the tough guy act is what he wants people to believe."

"I'll give you this, G," Vinnie said, "ain't nobody better at reading people than you are. What do you think happened with Albert and Borneo?" Vinnie asked.

"I don't know. But I think it must have been pretty serious for Borneo to have jumped in the river, given he can't swim a stroke."

Borneo and Albert were there like any Friday morning, looking a little rundown but otherwise okay. I noticed Albert seemed a little…nervous maybe. He was fidgety, but his eyes looked clear, and I couldn't smell the odor of alcohol.

"You guys okay?" I asked them.

"We're both fine," Borneo said. "Maybe a little worn out. We were up most of the night talking. We made a decision. We're going to start a group for veterans who came from the war not feeling right, for whatever reason. I don't know how that will go. It ain't easy for us soldiers to admit we got problems."

"That sounds great, Borneo," I said. "I hope you're going to be here on Labor Day. I sort of committed you to set pins for Mingo in his match against Peckham."

"We'll have to talk about that, G," Borneo said, "but we'll be here for a while. One thing about a band of brothers. We stick together."

"I think you're doing a good thing, Borneo," I said.

"Time for me and this old soldier Albert to rejoin the world." He turned to go to the cleaning closet. He stopped and looked back. "Thanks, G. Thanks for all you did."

CHAPTER 26

We were oiling the lanes when Frank came out of his office.

"This must be a momentous occasion," Vinnie said. "I don't think he's been out of that office twice this summer."

Frank stood near the shoe counter. "C'mere," he said. "Tomorrow is the third Saturday in August. You know what that means? It means it's the Travers Stakes. I go to the track once a year, and it's on Travers day. You know what else it means? You all get the day off. I can't trust you to keep this place running without me."

Vinnie and I looked at each other, stifling a laugh. Frank turned and went back to his office to read the *Daily News*.

"We have Saturday off," Vinnie said. "What do you think we should do?"

"Dunno," I said. "I'm sure we'll think of something."

But I had already thought of something. I just needed to figure it out.

It was miserable outside. Humid, and it felt like a storm was rolling in. The bowling alley was slow, and it was almost unbearable back in the cave when we had to set pins. My mom and Mrs. Antonioni brought sandwiches and a big jug of fresh lemonade for everyone. Sally looked at one sandwich and asked me what the meat was.

"Capicola," I said, "except when they say it, it sounds like *gabagool*. It's sort of a spicy ham. But it's good."

"I'll try it," Sally said.

"Take a piece of provolone to eat with it. It's a little strong, but I think you'll get to like it."

I grabbed a mortadella sandwich and said to Sally, "How about we go outside and eat down by the river?"

"Okay," she said.

"How do you like your capicola?" I asked.

"It's a little spicy for me," she said. "Do you eat this stuff all the time?"

"Not all the time," I said, "it's sort of a treat really. I'll trade if you want. Mortadella is just like baloney."

"No," she said, "I have a feeling if I'm going to stay in this town, I might be better off getting used to this stuff."

We both took a bite of our sandwiches. "What are you going to do with your day off?" I asked.

"I don't know. With all this working at the bowling alley and church and everything, I haven't had a chance to make many friends. I don't think you ever told me what your father does."

"He's a tailor," I said. "We may not be rich, but we have decent clothes."

"Is he from Italy?" Sally asked.

"Yes, both of my parents are from Italy. Near Florence. They came here after World War II. Their families lost everything in the war, and they decided to come to America. It just happened that both families landed in New York on the same day. I guess it was love at first sight. My mother told me that seems to run in our family." As soon as I said that, I wanted to take it back. Luckily, Sally didn't say anything.

"How did they wind up in Riverbend?" Sally asked.

"I guess they were on their way to Niagara Falls for their honeymoon. The train they were on broke down in Riverbend, and they spent a night here. They thought it was a beautiful setting for a town. Reminded them more of Tuscany than New York did. They moved up here a few months later." I took another bite of my sandwich. "It's been a little tough. With the town going downhill, there's not as much work for a good tailor. My pop's thinking about working in Albany. More fancy stores that sell suits to all the people who work at the state. Anyway, it's not so bad here I guess.

"You figured out where you are going to school?" I asked Sally.

"Only two choices," she said, "Most Precious Blood and the public junior high. My dad wouldn't ever consider Most Precious Blood, so I'll be at the public school."

"I was thinking about going to the movies tomorrow," I said. "I haven't seen a movie all summer. I can't go to the Mohawk 'cause they showed a condemned movie. They told us in church last Sunday. Then they made us take a pledge that we wouldn't ever go to any theater that showed condemned movies."

"You mean they showed a movie about someone who got the death penalty?" Sally said. "Why is that a problem?"

"No, a condemned movie means the Catholic Church doesn't approve of the movie because it's immoral. Seems like a lot of movies make that list. They post them in the back of the church. You can't go to a theater that shows immoral films."

"Your church seems to have a lot of power," Sally said. "So where can you go to the movies?"

"There's still the Bijou. Great double feature matinee tomorrow. *Herbie the Love Bug* and *101 Dalmatians*." I figured it was now or never. "Maybe we could go see it together."

"I don't think I can, G," Sally said. "I'm not allowed to date boys. My father says I am too young."

"It wouldn't be a date," I said. "We'd just be friends going to the movies."

"Well, we are friends," Sally said. "But I have to ask my father first. I couldn't just go without permission."

"Oh, sure," I said. "How about we meet there around twelve thirty. The movie starts at one."

"How about you come to my house at noon and meet my father. I'm sure he'd be happy to meet one of my friends."

"Sure," I stammered, "I'll see you tomorrow."

CHAPTER 27

Vinnie popped by at nine o'clock on Saturday. "C'mon, G, everyone's going to the park to play baseball."

"I don't know, Vinnie," I said. "Looks to me like it's gonna rain."

"Nah," he said. "Perfect day for baseball. And we've hardly gotten to play all summer."

"Okay," I said. "But I gotta be home by noon. I gotta help Pop with some stuff."

"What stuff? It's your day off."

"I don't know. Just stuff."

It didn't matter. By eleven, it was pouring, and we all headed home. I changed my clothes about five times and tried to figure out how to make my wavy hair look neat.

"Hey, Ma. Where's Pop keep the Vitalis?"

"Why you need Vitalis, Gianni?" she asked.

"Helps keep my hair in place," I said.

"Don't be a smart guy. You know what I'm asking."

"I'm going to the movies. I just want to look good," I said.

"Gianni Petrosino, what am I going to do with you? Look in the medicine cabinet in the bathroom."

Sally lived just west of the downtown on Division Street next to the First Presbyterian church. It was a small house, two stories with the front door recessed on the left side of the house so that there would be room for a long narrow front porch. I gathered myself and knocked on the door. A tall man in slacks and a white, short-sleeved button-down shirt answered the door. He looked through the screen door at me and said, "Hello, can I help you?"

I realized I hadn't prepared for the moment. "I'm Gianni Petrosino, but everyone calls me G."

"Johnny with a G. Okay. I'm Reverend Gibb. I'm still wondering how I might help you."

"Right," I said. "I'm here to take Sally to the matinee."

"Why don't you come in, Johnny with a G," and with that he opened the screen door.

"Pretty normal looking house you have here, Reverend," I said. "I mean, it looks like anyone's house. I mean, it doesn't look any different than most other houses I've seen."

He gave me a perplexed look. "Nice of you to notice, Mr. Petrosino," he said. "Sally told me you work together at the bowling alley."

"Yes, sir. We're pin boys," I said. "I mean we're pin boys and pin girls. Well, I'm not a pin girl but Sally is. The rest of us are pin boys."

"Thanks for clearing that up, Mr. Petrosino. Perhaps I can get you a glass of water while you're waiting."

"Yes, sir, that would be great." My throat had suddenly gone bone dry.

He brought the water to me, and I took a long drink. "Thank you, Reverend Gibb," I said.

"Sally talks about all you pin boys…and girl all the time. She tells me it is hard work, but everyone gets along well and supports each other. She hasn't had an opportunity to make a lot of friends, so I'm happy she has a job with such nice people."

"It's a great group," I said. "It's really hard work, but Charlie Horse… I mean, Sally holds her own."

"She also told me about her nickname."

Sally came down the stairs. She had a nice dress on and black leather shoes. "I see you met Gianni, Dad," she said.

"Yes. He seems like a nice young man. He also seemed very interested in the way our house looked."

Sally said, "I think it's the first time he's been inside a Presbyterian house," and laughed.

I said, "We better get going. The theater might be crowded since the weather isn't great. Plus, it's refrigerated. Great on a really hot, muggy summer day."

"You kids have a nice time at the movies," the Reverend said. "Sally, I'll expect you here for dinner."

CHAPTER 28

Vinnie and I walked home together as usual after the eleven o'clock mass.

Vinnie said, "I came back to get you after the rain stopped. Your pop answered the door and I asked for you. He said you had gone to the movies. I thought you had to help your pop with something?"

"I went to the double feature at the Bijou with Charlie Horse."

"And you didn't tell me? How long have we been friends that you gotta keep a secret from me?"

I felt a little embarrassed. "I just figured since we had the day off and I hadn't been to the movies for a while, it might be a fun thing. And I was eating my sandwich with Charlie Horse, and I just sort of asked her if she wanted to come. Otherwise, you know, I would have asked you."

"I'm hurt," Vinnie said. "So how was it?"

"The movie was funny. *Herbie the Love Bug*. It was about a car that does whatever it wants and wins big races."

Vinnie said, "Sounds pretty dumb to me. I don't think that movie will be making any money. So what happened with Charlie Horse? Did you make out?"

"We were just going as friends. There wasn't any making out," I said.

"C'mon, you can tell me. You don't go to the movies with a girl and just watch the movie," Vinnie said.

"There's nothing to tell, Vinnie. It was just something to do, that's all."

I thought about telling him, but I couldn't. We sat up in the balcony, toward the back. The theater wasn't that full, and we were pretty much by ourselves. I bought a bucket of popcorn, and Charlie

127

Horse bought sodas. The first movie was *101 Dalmatians*. I had seen it before, but it was still good. Our hands occasionally brushed in the popcorn bucket, but she didn't seem to react at all. I tried stretching once, and I thought maybe I could have my arm land on the back of her seat, but I chickened out.

The Love Bug was almost over, when she leaned over and kissed me quickly on the lips. "Thanks for taking me," she said.

"You're welcome," I replied.

And that was it. The movie was over, we left the theater, and I walked her home. It was just a peck, but at that moment, I knew it wasn't the banana oil at all. No, it was something more for sure.

Charlie Horse... Sally and I never had another date all through high school. She went to the public school, and I went to Most Precious Blood. She became popular in high school, and I did pretty well too, but the tradition was that the kids from the public school and the Catholic school didn't mix. We had our hangouts, they had theirs. We didn't even play each other in sports. Oh, Sally and I would see each other once in a while—Riverbend was too small not to find yourself in the same place at the same time—but we would usually just say hello and go on with whatever we were doing.

Of course, as it turned out, that one date stayed with us.

CHAPTER 29

Although we went to school with Crackers, we didn't know him very well. Even Vinnie, who knew everyone, hadn't really made friends with Crackers.

We had gotten to the bowling alley a little early on Monday. Crackers was sitting on one of the bowlers benches, nibbling saltines one at a time.

"How's it goin', Crackers," I said.

"Okay," he said.

"So why are you always eating saltines?" I asked. "Are they that good."

"Nah," he said, "I'm hungry all the time, and my mom thinks if I just eat saltines, I'll get full without putting on weight."

"Sounds like a good plan to me. How did you manage to wind up as a pin boy anyway?"

"My dad is Frank's dentist," Crackers said. "I guess he said he'd take care of his teeth for free if he gave me a job. I got the feeling Frank wasn't so excited about the idea once he saw me, but he kept his word and gave me the job." He ate another saltine.

"So do you like being a pin boy?" I asked.

"I think it's pretty hard work," he said. "But I like all the people back in the cave. I guess I never thought I'd get to know you and Vinnie because you were the cool people."

"Ah, we're not any cooler than anybody else, Crackers," I said. "But you know Vinnie. To him everybody is just a friend he hasn't made yet. What's your favorite class?"

"Geography," he said. "I think it is fun to learn about different places. One of these days, I'm going to travel all over the world."

"Which one do you like the least?" I asked.

"That's easy," he laughed. "Gym. I'm always the last one picked for everything. The worst game is dodgeball. I'm a pretty big target, and most of the kids seem to enjoy picking on me."

I felt sheepish. There was probably a time or two Vinnie and I laughed at him along with everyone else. "I think you're a pretty good pin boy," I said. "I don't think anyone works any harder."

"Thanks, G. It's different back in the cave. No one makes fun of me, and I don't feel like the weird kid with you guys," he said. He munched another saltine. "It's not like I'm trying to be fat. My mom watches everything I eat. 'Course when yours and Vinnie's mom brings in Italian food, I can't resist it. Otherwise, I have more cottage cheese and saltines than any kid in history. Doesn't seem to make any difference though. Every year, I seem to get a little bigger. My grandma says I'm just big-boned. Says it runs in the family."

"Doesn't your family go to the eleven o'clock mass on Sunday?" I said.

"Usually. Sometimes we go earlier, but my mom likes the high mass with the chanting and the extra candles."

"Listen. Me and Vinnie usually like to hang out a little bit after mass, before we have to be home for Sunday dinner. You want to hang out with us next Sunday?"

Crackers lit up. "You mean it? You wouldn't mind being seen with me?"

"That's a dumb thing to say," I laughed. "You can hang out with us anytime you want. In fact, at school this year, you can eat lunch with us if you want too."

"Really? You're not kidding?" he said.

"Crackers, we're friends. And that's what friends do. They hang out together. Don't let anyone ever tell you any different."

CHAPTER 30

The match was only a week away, and Tony Gallo still had some final preparations. He figured he had bought most of the available clams on the east coast, and a truckload of oyster crackers and cocktail sauce to go with them. He put himself in charge of the *sufreit*, a stew made with things like hearts and lungs. It didn't taste bad as long as nobody told you what you were eating. He had local farmers delivering all the fresh corn they had left in the field. He figured Lombardo would be making Italian sausage and *kielbasa* all week, and there would be plenty of hamburgers and hot dogs for anyone who would rather eat that than sausage and peppers. And of course, the liquor would flow courtesy of Tommy Spagnolo, the biggest distributor in the area.

The local softball players were peeved at Tony for taking over the entire Veteran's Field, but he bought them off with free tickets to the event. Of course, he had signed off on the permit himself, as if he really needed one. He had the pavilion set up with poker tables, two craps tables, a birdcage, and wheel of fortune. He was smart enough to give the entire police department free tickets as well, making sure they wouldn't do more than take care of anybody who got out of hand. He didn't figure to make much money on the gambling, but he thought between that and the ticket sales, he could at least pay for the food.

Tony went through the invitation list. He had gotten affirmative replies from all the important politicians in the area, including the longtime Congressman Stan Braxton. Braxton seemed to be wavering about supporting federal funding for all the roadwork that needed to be done for his downtown mall and the new, wider bridge across the Mohawk that would need to be built to shuttle people into Riverbend from the Thruway. Once Braxton saw the enthusiasm for Riverbend, Tony would get all the money he needed.

He thought long and hard about inviting Giuseppe Simone, but in the end decided it never hurt to have a friend like that in his back pocket. He said he would put up a thousand dollars on Mingo in Giuseppe's name and hand him the winnings after the match. He'd tell Paulie about the deal with Simone later this week.

Tony also had a group of investors coming to the clambake. It bothered him that he wouldn't have a lot of time to throw craps, but he needed to make sure he had commitments from them before they left town. He figured it didn't hurt to have some help available just in case.

And Tony had one more surprise up his sleeve. He managed to get Ed Ames, Mingo from the Daniel Boone TV show, to make an appearance. It cost him five grand, but he was going to set up a hatchet throwing booth where people could test their skill against the real Mingo.

Tony made one more trip to the bowling alley. He decided it wasn't worth repainting, but he got a crew from the public works department to scrub the place from floor to ceiling and the highway shop to spruce up the bowling alley sign. He had a big banner made to hang at the bowling alley and a welcome sign to hang at Veteran's Field with the names of all the important people who would be in town.

Tony still had two calls to make. First, he called Jacky Di Felipo.

"Jacky, *paisan*, how's every little thing?" Tony said.

"Tony, couldn't be better. Not only is PG winning every match, he's doing it with style. We finish this Friday in Yonkers, and we'll drive up on Sunday. When he hits Riverbend, he'll make sure to make a splash. I figure the people will bet Mingo either because they won't be able to stand PG or because the odds ought to be juicy."

"One other thing," Tony said. "Keep PG sober on Monday. I can't have people thinking he lost because of all the Chivas Regal he'll want to down."

Jacky said, "No worries. I'll be his good shepherd."

"I know I can count on you, Jacky," Tony said. "Come see me first thing you get here on Sunday. I'll be at the golf course."

Tony felt confident in Jacky. He wasn't as sure about Paulie. He dialed the number to Paulie's store. Tony Sharp answered.

"This is Tony Gallo. Put Paulie on the line."

Tony heard some shuffling, and then Paulie picked up the phone. "Yeah," he said.

"Paulie, it's Tony. Just making sure everything is ready to go. Oh, and one more thing. I got Giuseppe Simone down for a thousand dollars. You'll have to cover that too."

"It's been a good August, Tony, but this match could break me. You better know what you are doing. And one more thing. This favor cleans my slate. From this point on we're even."

Tony scratched his chin and measured his words. "Paulie, let me remind you of two things. First, the only reason your business is as good as it is, is because I make sure you get all the action from Riverbend and most of everything else from Albany to Utica."

"You know I appreciate your help, Tony," Paulie said, "but I put a lot of hard work into this business." He paused. "What's the second thing?"

"The second thing is that we're even when I say we're even." Tony softened his tone. "Paulie, you and me don't need to fight. We've been good for each other for a lot of years. No reason that ever has to change. You just hold up your end, and I promise you you'll make more money than you ever dreamed of. One thing you know about me. I always take care of my friends…and my enemies too."

Paulie backed down. "I know that, Tony. I'm just a little nervous. It's a lot of money for me. It'd be a lot of money for anyone. Don't worry. I'll hold up my end."

"Good. Don't worry, I understand your worries, but I got this totally thought out. We're all going to come out of this on top. Especially Riverbend. Hell, Paulie, you may even be able to go totally legit after this. Start gambling with the real crooks on the stock market." Tony let out a big laugh. Paulie just gritted his teeth.

"Just call me if you have any problems, Paulie. I'll talk with you soon." Tony said.

Tony thought about what Paulie said. Nobody threatens to run out on Tony Gallo. But now wasn't the time to deal with it. He'd take care of Paulie once the match was over.

CHAPTER 31

David Greene was sitting in a booth at the Colonie Diner, drinking a cup of coffee and moving some scrambled eggs around his plate. He wasn't very hungry but figured he couldn't take up space without ordering. Two men in slacks and golf shirts slid in across from him.

"Mayor Greene? We're from the State Bureau of Criminal Investigations. We'd like to talk with you about Tony Gallo."

"You guys got some ID? I mean, aren't you guys required to wear cheap suits and sunglasses?"

They both pulled out their badges. "I'm Detective James, this is Detective Bennett. This is not a joke mayor. I'd advise you to take this seriously."

"Okay, fellas. Sorry about that. So what do you want to talk with me about?" Greene said.

"We can't give you specifics, of course, but we've had our eye on Tony Gallo for some time now. For a while, we weren't sure you weren't part of his schemes, but based on all the information we've gathered, we think you're clean. In fact, we think you'd like nothing better than to see Tony Gallo out of your hair. Do we have that right, Mayor Greene?"

"Ahhh… I really don't know anything about most of what Tony does. Except for this whole bowling thing. He has this idea that we're going to hold a bowling match, and it's going to save Riverbend."

James and Bennett looked at each other. Bennett said, "A bowling match?"

"Yeah, Mingo against P. G. Peckham," Greene said.

"Mingo? Daniel Boone's sidekick?" Bennett said.

135

"Well, he's going to be there too, but no, it's Riverbend's Mingo who is going to bowl," Greene said.

"We'll have to worry about that another time, Mayor. We have bigger things on our plate. We hear the financial situation in Riverbend isn't so good."

Greene said, "I know we're so broke we couldn't afford one of Wortham's old brooms. What's that got to do with Tony?

James said, "Well, we don't think Riverbend's dire situation is entirely the fault of too much spending and too little revenue. We think Tony Gallo might be...helping the situation along."

Greene was almost giddy. "Just tell me what you need. You have my full cooperation."

CHAPTER 32

The weather was perfect on Labor Day. Sunny, mid-seventies, low humidity, just a mild breeze. Tony Gallo was out of the house and on his way to Veteran's Field by seven. People would probably start showing up around eleven, and he wanted to make sure everything was ready. He had gone out to dinner the previous night with Jacky Di Felipo and P. G. Peckham. He wondered how anyone could stand Peckham and gave Jacky credit for being able to travel around the east coast with him.

Tony doled out *sufreit* most of the morning. David Greene showed up at noon. "You seem particularly happy this morning, Mayor," Tony said.

"I am happy. For the first time in a long time, I feel like there is a light at the end of the tunnel."

"I knew you'd come around to my way of thinking, Davey. Everything is going to be just fine."

"When you're right, you're right, Tony. I think come tomorrow, we'll be looking at the new Riverbend." Greene walked away laughing.

What an asshole, Tony thought. There would be a new Riverbend, but David Greene wouldn't have anything to do with it.

CHAPTER 33

Vinnie and I were at the bowling alley by ten as usual.

Yakky caught us as soon as we came in. "No bowling today, fellas. We'll get the lanes oiled up around five so be back then. Meanwhile, go enjoy the clambake. I might be up there myself in a couple of hours. Just a few things I need to take care of here first."

We started up the hill to Veteran's Field. "You ever been to a clambake before?" Vinnie asked.

"Last year," I said. "My pop took me. They had a special softball game. The King and his Court. They played against the best players in Riverbend. They only had four players—a pitcher, catcher, first baseman, and shortstop. The pitcher was amazing. He struck out players throwing from second base, behind his back, between his legs, even blindfolded. They said he struck out Willie Mays, Willie McCovey, Brooks Robinson, Maury Wills, Harmon Killebrew, and Roberto Clemente in a row. They beat the Riverbend team 13–5. It just seemed when he decided to put someone away, he did it. It was a lot of fun. And the food was great. They had something called *sufreit*. They never told me what was in it, but it wasn't bad. When my pop saw me eating it, he laughed. I asked what he thought was so funny, but he just said he'd tell me sometime. The whole thing went on until late. I didn't get home until eleven thirty. My ma was pretty upset at Pop, but he told her it was time for me to spend some time with the men."

We made it to the park in about fifteen minutes. A man at the gate said, "You boys have tickets?"

"No, how much are they?" I asked.

Paulie DiMeo came up behind us. "I'll take care of these boys," he said.

"Thanks, Paulie," Vinnie said.

"You think maybe when you're done at the bowling alley you might come back and help me out?" Paulie said.

"I don't know, Paulie," Vinnie said, "my pop doesn't think that's a respectable job for an Antonioni."

"You think about it, Vinnie. Talent like yours comes along once in a while. Hate to see it wasted."

We wandered around a bit. Vinnie tried some *sufreit* and said it tasted pretty strange. We found the hatchet throwing area. Sure enough, Ed Ames was there, signing autographs and taking pictures with people. They kept us out of the pavilion—adults only, they said. They had brought in some carnival games, and Vinnie and I lost about five dollars each. We headed back to the bowling alley at four thirty.

Everyone was there. Danny had the banana oil and the mops out.

Charlie Horse said, "Mingo and Peckham just left. They were just getting a little bit of practice in. Peckham was unmerciful to Mingo. Doing some Indian war hoots and needling him non-stop. It was pretty enjoyable."

Borneo said, "Let's get this place ready. We'll be using lanes three and four, so that's the only ones we'll have to oil. Vinnie, you and G take care of oiling. Albert, Crackers, and Charlie Horse can set up the chairs for the spectators. Danny and I will go back to the cave and pick out the twenty best pins. Showtime is nine o'clock. Let's have the place ready by seven. It's our big night. Let's show 'em what we can do."

CHAPTER 34

Mingo got up around noon. He figured he hadn't slept more than two hours total. He thought maybe he'd go see if he could practice in the afternoon. Tony Gallo told him to be at Veteran's Field by one o'clock so he could meet Peckham. He figured maybe an hour of that and he could still get an hour of practice in. He washed, dressed, and drove the 88 up to Veteran's Field. He saw Tony at the pavilion with P. G. Peckham and Jacky Di Felipo. He could immediately spot Peckham. Button-down western shirt with cowboys on bucking broncos all over it, blue tinted granny glasses, and bell-bottom pants that must have flared twelve inches at the bottom. He walked toward them.

Peckham spoke first. "You must be the famous Mungo. I hear you're supposed to be a great bowler. If that's so, why aren't you out there with the rest of us on the tour? Well, if you figure on beating ole P. G. Peckham first, you just might be disappointed."

"It's Mingo, not Mungo, Mr. Peckham. And I know you're a great bowler. But I think maybe I can beat you. Least I'm gonna try."

Tony spoke up. "Hey, fellas, save it for the match. C'mon up with me to the stage. I'm gonna introduce you two."

Tony had a microphone ready. "S'cuse me, gentlemen, but I have an important announcement to make. We have with us today two of the finest bowlers in the world. The incomparable P. G. Peckham from Buffalo and our own Marcus Aurelius Pandolfo, Mingo, and tonight they are going to put on a bowling match the likes of which Riverbend has never seen before. Let's give our two bowlers a big hand."

The crowd obviously wanted to go back to their gambling but knew better than to ignore Tony Gallo. The cheers weren't exactly overwhelming, but they were enthusiastic enough.

Peckham took the microphone from Tony. "I just want you people to know I won't rough up your boy too bad tonight. But you can count on me beating him 'cause P. G. Peckham don't plan on getting beat by some hick from the sticks. So you all come out tonight and watch the match. And if you're smart, you'll put your money on Peckham. I'm in such a good mood, I might even bowl a perfect game tonight. After all, that's why they call me PG. Hey there, Mungo, you got anything you want to say before I give that microphone back to Tony? Anything at all? Maybe ask him if you can get out of getting whooped tonight?" He shoved the microphone at Mingo, and for one of the very few times in his life, Mingo seemed short of words.

"I got nothing much to say except you better bowl the best set of your life 'cause I don't plan on losing." And with that, he gave the microphone back to Tony.

Tony grinned wide, the gap in his teeth prominently marking the middle of his mouth. "You heard 'em, boys. Gonna be the match of the century right here in Riverbend, tonight at nine o'clock at Riverbend Alleys. C'mon down and root Riverbend's favorite son on to victory."

Tony let them go back to their card playing. "Jacky, you and Peckham better take off before anything gets out of hand. I've got some other people to see this afternoon, but I'll see you tonight at the bowling alley. Just remember, we have a deal."

Tony found Stan Braxton holding court at the bar. "Tony, Tony, my man," Braxton said. "How's Riverbend's hardest working citizen?"

"I'm doing good, Stan. You're looking aces. Helluva tan you got. You been spending time out on the course?" Tony said.

"Maybe a round here and there," Braxton said. "Great party you put on, Tony. Looks like most of Riverbend showed up."

"I'm telling you, Stan, the people who live here love the town. We all just want to see it prosper. You can be a big help to us. Once we put our mall downtown, we'll need a lot of roadwork done. And you know as well as I do that the old bridge is an accident waiting to happen. You know we can't do it without your help." Tony looked straight at him. "You know as well as I do that most of these people voted for you. They contributed to your campaigns. They knocked on doors for you. We haven't asked for much in return."

"You don't think I know all that? Hell, if I can't return some federal money to my constituents, what good would I be as a congressman?" This time Braxton looked right at Tony. "You'll get your federal money, but I need a favor from you. One hand washes the other, Tony. You've always known that."

"You know you don't have to muscle me, Stan. All you have to do is ask."

"Don't misconstrue me, Tony. I know that. Just letting you know I need your help as much as you need mine. Things have been a little tight for me lately. Some bad investments as it were. I could use a winner, and I'm thinking maybe this whole bridge thing might be a good place to find one. See, my kid is working for Vitale Construction. I know they'd do a great job on the bridge. And I know they'd be thankful to both of us for the work, if you catch my drift. My job is to get you the federal money. Your job is to make sure it gets spent in the right way."

"Stan, how long have we known each other?" Tony asked.

"I don't know, Tony. Thirty years maybe. Why?"

"Just wondering when in thirty years I've let you down. You don't get elected to Congress that many times without help."

"Don't take offense, Tony. I never doubted you for a minute. You can count on me."

Tony grabbed Braxton's hand. Braxton almost looked lost in Tony's oversized meat hook.

"Always good doing business with you, Stan," Tony said. "I've got to talk to some other people. Get some of my *sufreit*. It's the best you'll ever eat."

Tony found Giuseppe Simone at one of the craps tables.

"You winning, *paisan*?" Tony asked.

Simone winked. "Maybe a few bucks."

"Good, good," Tony said. "Don't let me disturb you. Get back to winning money. But remember to see me before the match. I got a special seat for you tonight."

Tony looked for Paulie. He found him at one of the poker tables. "Paulie, have a minute of your time?"

"Deal me out of this one, fellas," Paulie said. "Sure, Tony. Let's take a walk."

They headed out across the field, toward the city swimming pool.

"You doing good, Paulie?" Tony asked.

"Never been better, Tony."

"*Molto buona*, Paulie. Just making sure everything is set. How's the action looking?"

"I got Mingo at plus 370, Peckham at minus 400. The action is still running pretty heavy in favor of Peckham."

Tony looked irritated. "Sure it is. You're barely giving a fair return on Mingo. Course you haven't seen the bets from Giuseppe Simone and Stan Braxton yet. That might even it out a bit. Still, you might think about jumping Mingo up a little before the match. I'm sure all the Mingo backers will appreciate the return."

"I'll think about it, Tony. I'm just trying to break even."

"Beautiful day," Tony said. "More ways than one. Let's get back to the clambake. I'm feeling like a sausage sandwich."

CHAPTER 35

Mingo got to the bowling alley a little after three. Yakky was behind the counter.

"I'm going to roll a few lines, Yakky," said Mingo, "just to warm up."

"I wouldn't care, but we don't have any pin boys back there. Why don't you let me see if I can find Albert or Danny."

Yakky went out back to see if Albert was sitting under one of the trees drinking his beer out of a paper bag. Mingo sat on one of the benches and stared down the lane, wondering how he could possibly beat Peckham. He heard the front door open and turned to see Peckham coming in.

"Guess you had the same idea, Mingo. I always like to test out the lanes before a match. They're all different, you know. Oh, same length, same width, but they all feel different. It's sort of like sighting a gun." Peckham took his blue glasses off and pulled a T-shirt out of his bag.

"It wasn't that for me," Mingo said, "I just needed to work off some nervous energy. I've bowled on these lanes a thousand times at least. I know every board, from the rock maple to the pine to the pin deck. No, I'm not worried about these lanes. You ever bowl with pin boys, PG?"

"Nope. Never anything but automatic pinsetters. Is it that different?" Peckham asked.

"It's better. You never have to worry about a wobbling pin getting gobbled up by the machine. And the pins are set in the same place every time, just like the machine."

Peckham said, "You're not worried are you, Mingo? Tony Gallo's got this all figured out. How much you getting when you win?"

144

"When I win? What do you mean when I win? I'm not getting anything except a chance to get out of here."

Peckham realized that Mingo wasn't in on the deal. "You don't know, do you? You're gonna win. It's all set up. I mean, I'm gonna bowl close to my best, but in the end, you'll be the winner. Get used to the idea. You're going to be like if one of the Clanton's outdrew Wyatt Earp. You're gonna be famous. The kid who knocked off Peckham. It's your big break. Don't look a gift horse in the mouth."

"I can't be part of that. I don't want to win that way. I'm only going to bowl if you promise to do your best," Mingo said.

"Don't be a fool, kid. There's too many people with too much riding on this. You're gonna bowl, and you're gonna win. You ever think what might happen if you don't?" Peckham took a deep breath. "Tell you what. I'll promise the first two games I won't pull any punches as long as you give me the best you got. You and I will know who's the best. You got two games to beat me straight up. And we'll see about the third game. I don't like getting beat. Everyone knows that. I'm not even sure I can miss if I have to. What do you say, Mingo?"

"I gotta think about it," Mingo said.

"Don't think about it too long," Peckham said. "We'll be bowling in a couple of hours."

Mingo stared back down the lane. It was too late now to say anything. He knew he had to go through with the match. He did like Peckham's sense of fair play though. He would bowl the first two games fair and square. He'd still know who the best bowler was.

Yakky found Albert sitting under the tree, but he was drinking a bottle of orange soda. Crackers was sitting with him eating a package of saltines.

"You guys want to earn a few extra dollars? I think I can get Peckham and Mingo to give you each ten bucks for an hour's work. What do you say?"

"Why not," Albert said. "What do you say, Crackers?"

Crackers just nodded, got up, and brushed his pants off.

Yakky came through the door with Albert and Crackers just as Mingo and Peckham had gotten done talking. "Got us a couple of pin boys. You guys can have the lanes to yourself for an hour or so. Oh, you'll owe them ten bucks each. Pay after you're done."

Peckham changed his shirt, put on his bowling shoes and his blue glasses, took his ball out of the bag, and got ready to bowl. Albert had the pins set on lane three. Peckham approached the line, let the ball go, and all tenpins went flying.

"I think I'm gonna like this place," Peckham said. "You know what they say, Mingo. May the best man win."

CHAPTER 36

Riverbend Alleys was cramped, and they did well to fit two hundred people inside. A much bigger crowd had gathered outside, and it was decided that Charlie Horse would go back and forth to provide updates.

Borneo gathered the pin boys together at eight thirty. "I've got nothing more to say. Far as I'm concerned, it's just another day at the alleys. Danny and I will handle the pins. We're taking Crackers and Albert back to the cave with us just in case one of us gets caught by a flying pin. G, you watch the foul line. Vinnie, you back G up, just in case there is any question. Charlie Horse, you'll be running outside to give the crowd updates. Anybody got any questions?"

The other pin boys didn't say a word.

Borneo said, "All right then, let's go."

Mingo and Peckham started warming up at around 8:45. Peckham wore a black shirt with two red thunderbirds on the front of each shoulder and a large red PG on the back, tan slacks, and white bowling shoes with black lines on the side. Definitely looking the part of the bad guy. Mingo was wearing a shirt colored red, white, and green, brown slacks, and his usual red, white, and green bowling shoes.

The difference in their bowling styles was glaring. Peckham used the full sixteen-pound ball most of the professional bowlers used. For a man of his slight stature sixteen pounds may have seemed too heavy, but Peckham's muscled right arm had long since gotten used to throwing it. Peckham took a normal five-step approach but started from far on the left side of the lane. He would swing his arm back so far his blue rubber ball would be over his head, following through with all the strength his slight body could muster. He imparted a violent sideways spin across the oiled part of the lane, looking for sure as if the ball would go straight into the right hand gutter, before catching the dry wood and curving perfectly into the 1-3 pocket. The force of throwing the heavy ball caused him to look as if he would lose his balance and go flying down the lane himself, but he caught himself every time, turning and walking back before the pins scattered.

Mingo had a classic delivery. He set up just left of the center of the lane, back straight, shoulders centered squarely to the target, knees slightly bent. He held his ball at about even with his belly button just off to the side, right hand underneath the ball, left hand helping to steady it. He took the same five-step approach as Peckham, only smoother, swinging back to shoulder height and releasing the ball to roll between the first and second arrow on the lane with just enough curve to catch the pocket squarely. In comparison to Peckham, his throw looked effortless. When he finished, he was posed almost like a ballerina at the end of a dance.

At exactly nine o'clock, Peckham and Mingo sat down, and Yakky spoke into the microphone for everyone to settle down. Yakky was a natural announcer.

"Ladies and gentlemen," he started, although there weren't more than five women in the place including Mingo's mother, "welcome to the match of the century right here at Riverbend Alleys. Tonight, you are all privileged to watch the greatest bowler in the world, P. G. Peckham, face off against the best bowler Riverbend's ever produced, Marcus Aurelius Pandolfo, the one and only Mingo." The crowd erupted in enthusiastic applause.

Yakky continued. "Settle down, settle down. We'll use all the rules of the Professional Bowlers Association. Both you bowlers know what they are. Now remember, each bowler needs to stay seated behind his competitor while he is bowling. Make sure you only use your own ball to bowl. Watch the foul line. You go across it and that ball counts for zero. Oh, and keep the swearing and bad language down…as much as possible anyway.

"The format is simple. The match will consist of three games. The total score of the three games for each bowler determines the winner. Doesn't matter who wins each game, only the total pins for the three games. There will be a five-minute rest period between games. Mingo won the coin toss, so he'll lead off in the first and third games. The bowler who leads off will bowl one frame and after that, each bowler will bowl two frames when it is his turn. Okay. If everyone's ready, let's bowl."

CHAPTER 37

The pins were set. G was ready. Mingo got up out of his seat and picked his ball out of the tray. The crowd was totally silent. Mingo lined up on lane 3, took his approach, let the ball go, and nailed the pocket, sending all tenpins flying. The crowd erupted, and Mingo sat down, breathing a huge sigh of relief. Peckham looked at him. "Guess you're serious here, Mingo. Always good to get that first one out of the way."

Peckham moved over to the left side of the lane, looked like he was going to make an approach, and suddenly just hung the ball down and looked at the crowd and said in a loud voice, "You people gonna keep moving all night? Didn't anybody let you know there was a bowling match going on? Sit still in your seats."

Vinnie and I looked at each other. As far as we could tell, no one had moved a muscle.

Peckham got done glaring at the crowd and reset himself. Five steps and a fling, and just before the ball was going to fall into the gutter, it curved into the pins. A strike for Peckham. He turned to the crowd and made a motion with his fingers like they were shooting six-guns, and once he had finished firing, he blew the imaginary smoke off of the barrels.

He strutted back to the ball return and picked his ball out. He hit a little high in the pocket and left the five and eight pins. Just before he was ready to pick up the spare, he turned the crowd again. "You people just don't learn. I guess here in Hicktown, they don't know the meaning of stop moving when I'm making my approach." He turned back and easily picked up the spare.

Mingo waited until Peckham had taken his seat, but before he could bowl, Peckham looked at the crowd and said, "Don't you have

150

any women in this town? Why you hiding them all? You afraid they might be tempted to leave with me?"

Mingo did his best to zone him out but left a solid tenpin. He picked up the spare and moved over to lane three. Another perfect roll and another strike.

Peckham smiled at Mingo and grabbed his ball. He stood at the head of the lane and started gyrating his hips. "You ever seen anyone move so good as me? I'm not only pretty, I'm the best dancer you ever seen." Then he looked at the crowd again, and said, "And if you don't stop moving I'm gonna come over there and make you stop moving." He flung the ball down the lane, gyrated a little more and left the nine pin. He picked up the spare and looked at Mingo. "This one's for you, the best bowler in Riverbend," and added another strike. "You better pick it up, Mingo, I'm feeling it tonight."

Mingo responded with a strike of his own, left the tenpin on the next ball, and hit it squarely for his spare. Peckham left the tenpin on his next ball, made the spare, and then rolled three straight strikes. Mingo left one pin on each of his next two rolls but easily converted the spares, following those with a solid strike in the eighth frame. After eight frames, Mingo had a potential 177, Peckham a potential 188. Peckham left the four pin in the ninth frame, and in the tenth left a solid tenpin, converting the spare and finishing the game with a strike for 217. Mingo rolled a strike in the ninth and on his first ball in the tenth frame, finishing by knocking down all the pins except for the seven and picking up the spare for a total of 226. A nine pin lead going into the second game. They each had six strikes, but Mingo made his count more by stringing them together.

Tony Gallo leaned over to Jacky Di Felipo. "Very nice, Jacky. He looked to me like he was putting all he had into it. Is he always such a *stronzo*?"

"You gotta hand it to him. He knows how to work a crowd," Jacky said.

Which seemed to be Peckham's cue to put his five-minute break to good use. Peckham wandered over to the crowd and said, "You ain't seen nothin' yet. I gave your boy a break that game, but all of you who have bets on him better get used to the idea that it's gone money. Even all your moving around and talking can't stop Peckham. You know why? 'Cause I'm the best there ever was. Not second or third best. Number one. Top of the heap." His voice rose a few decibels. "I got here all by myself. You didn't do anything for me. You should all be thankful you're getting a chance to see me in my prime. Nobody has the Peckham style."

Vinnie went over to Mingo. "Nice game. Keep it up, and you'll beat him."

Mingo said, "It's not the bowling. It's having to watch him prance around like a chicken and cluck at the crowd."

Vinnie said, "Yeah, that never happens when you bowl," and then rolled his eyes. Mingo glared at him. "Keep it up, Mingo," Vinnie said. He came back to where G was calling fouls. "Anyone ever get close to the foul line?"

"Close, but never over," I said. "They just set up in the exact right spot every time. Second game is about to start."

Both players started with strikes. Through the first five frames, Peckham had two strikes and three spares and a score of 99. Mingo was throwing the ball consistently and had four strikes to go along with a spare in the second frame, giving him almost a thirty pin advantage, but in the sixth frame disaster struck with the dreaded 7-10 split. Mingo picked off the seven pin giving him a score of 126 in the sixth frame and letting Peckham back into the match. Peckham took advantage with strikes in the next two frames, a spare, and another strike in the ninth frame.

Mingo recovered slightly but still only finished with a score of 205. Peckham managed to pick up 18 pins in the tenth frame for a score of 212.

Mingo felt a rush knowing he had beaten Peckham straight up, but he could have all but put him away had he not had an open frame. Peckham kept up his running battle with the crowd and showed no signs of getting tired of the act. Peckham slid over to where Mingo was sitting and said, "Nice going. Two pin difference. I figured the advantage you have with this being your home lanes must have been about tenpins, so I'm thinking straight up I beat you by eight. Of course, I've been thinking, we have such a great match going we ought to just play this third game straight up. Whadda you say? Think your best can take my best?"

Peckham was still a bundle of energy while Mingo looked close to drained. Mingo said, "I came here to win, but I want to win fair and square. I'm good enough to beat you straight up. Go ahead and give me your best."

Peckham said, "Be careful what you ask for. You just remember, anytime I want I can bury you or anyone else they throw against me. I believe you're leading off this game. Go ahead. It's your big moment."

Back in the cave, Borneo and Danny felt the same pressure. "Mingo is up by two pins," Borneo said. "He's got a chance to win. Danny, you've got to do your best this game. It's the biggest game Riverbend's ever seen."

"I will, Borneo. I'll do my best."

"I know you will, Danny. Albert, Crackers, you guys stay sharp. Never know when one of us might get hit with a flying pin."

Mingo led off the third game with a strike. Peckham responded with a double. Mingo left a solid tenpin and picked up the spare, following that with a strike. Peckham threw a third strike, left the seven pin, and easily clipped it for the spare. Mingo doubled with a strike in the fourth frame, left the six pin on the next ball, and made the spare. Peckham threw a perfect strike in the fifth frame, left a wobbly tenpin in the sixth, and picked it up. Mingo left two solid tenpins on the next two frames, picking up the spare each time. Peckham looked like he was feeling it and came back with two strikes in the seventh and eighth frames. Mingo responded with a strike in his eighth frame but left the stubborn tenpin again in the ninth.

Peckham had two frames to go. All he needed to do was mark in the ninth and tenth and Mingo was shut out. A spare in the ninth and twenty pins in the tenth would give him a score in the high 220s. Even if Mingo rolled three strikes in the tenth frame the best he could do was 217.

Peckham saw that the crowd had deflated. He turned to them and said, "Too bad your boy wasn't just a little bit better. But who beats the greatest? Nobody, that's who. All you people who bet on P.

G. Peckham get in the collection line." He turned to Mingo. "Say goodnight, Mingo. It's all over." And then he winked at Mingo. It was subtle, but Mingo figured he was telling him, don't worry, you're still going to win.

Jacky Di Felipo was hunched over in his seat. Tony leaned over to him and said, "This isn't looking good, Jacky. Mingo is about shut out."

"Don't worry, Tony," Jacky said. "Peckham knows the score."

"He better. The score is zero for you if Mingo don't win."

Tony looked over at Giuseppe Simone. Simone was stone-faced. The only one who seemed to be smiling was David Greene. Tony wondered why since he wouldn't even gamble on penny ante poker.

Peckham's ninth frame was like slow motion to Mingo. He barely heard the crowd, which by this time was handing it back to Peckham as much as he was giving it. Peckham let the ball go, and it crashed dead into the center of the headpin, leaving the 7-10 split. Peckham started jumping up and down, screaming at the crowd, "I told you yokels to sit still. How stupid are you that you can't even follow a simple request. It's your fault. Who's the referee for this match? I want that frame over. You can't cheat me out of my victory."

Everyone looked at Yakky. He wasn't sure how he got to be the match referee, but he said, "Nobody interfered with your frame. The throw stands."

The four pin boys in the cave were wondering what all the commotion was about. Borneo said, "I didn't think I would ever find a bowler who was a bigger jerk than Mingo, but I think P. G. Peckham might get the award."

Peckham wouldn't give up. "That's the only way he can win. You got this whole town against me." After five more minutes of ranting, Peckham picked up his ball and knocked down the seven pin. He rolled a strike and a spare in the tenth frame to finish at 215.

Tony Gallo allowed himself a gap-toothed smile. He looked directly at Mingo, but Mingo wouldn't return his glance. There was a battle going on inside Mingo. This was it. His big chance. Why shouldn't he win? He beat Peckham in the first two games when they were both trying their best. He deserved to win. Peckham just threw a bad ball. We've all done it, he thought. This wasn't about Riverbend. It was about him. It was his moment.

Peckham slumped in his seat, although Mingo saw what for sure was a little grin. The crowd was deathly silent. Mingo grabbed his ball, approached the lane, and threw a strike. The crowd erupted, and Mingo allowed himself a small fist-pump. He waited for them to settle down, retrieved his ball, and threw a second strike. The crowd went wild. Chants of "C'mon, Mingo" and "You can do it, Mingo" circulated through the crowd.

With the first two strikes, he was sitting at 207. He only needed six pins to tie the match, almost a certainty. Anything more than that and he would win. He looked at Vinnie and G. G mouthed, bowl a strike. He looked at Tony Gallo with his big grin. He looked at Peckham who seemed pretty smug for a guy who was going to lose the match.

The crowd quieted. Mingo seemed to pause an extra ten seconds at the head of the lane, and then he put his ball down, went back to his seat, and took a drink.

"Pressure can make a guy pretty dry, eh, Mingo," Peckham said. Mingo finished his swig and went back to the lane. He set up and instead of focusing totally on the pins, he glanced quickly at me. I wasn't certain, but I thought Mingo was set up just slightly ahead of his normal spot. Mingo turned back, made his approach and let the ball go.

It was a perfect strike. The crowd was on its feet, yelling. Charlie Horse ran outside to announce the victory. It was then that Yakky noticed I had my hand in the air.

"Wait, wait," he yelled, trying to get the crowd to calm down. "Everybody, be quiet. Everybody stop yelling."

Peckham had gotten up to shake Mingo's hand, but Mingo didn't stick his hand out. Peckham, who might have had the loudest voice of all yelled, "Everybody shut up. The referee wants to make this thing official."

The crowd noise was reduced to a few murmurs.

Yakky looked at me. I said, "His left foot went over the foul line." Going over the line meant that the shot would count as zero.

The crowd erupted again. "No way, the kid doesn't know what he's talking about."

Peckham yelled, "I saw him, he didn't go over the line. It was a good roll. He won fair and square."

Tony Gallo went up to Yakky and whispered something. Yakky said, "Since Mr. Peckham is satisfied, and we don't have anyone else who saw it, I think we should declare Mingo the winner."

Vinnie spoke up. "I saw it too. He fouled."

The crowd was having none of it. "Mingo wins," they started chanting.

And at that point, Mingo said, "Everybody settle down. I've got something to say."

The crowd calmed down once more.

Mingo said, "G was right. I went over the foul line. It wasn't by much, but I fouled. Peckham wins the match."

The crowd was stunned. It was at that point that Mingo stuck his hand out to shake Peckham's. Peckham weakly responded, and as the two competitors were shaking hands, a group of uniformed men with guns burst through the door.

"Nobody move! State Bureau of Criminal Investigation!"

EPILOGUE

I had time to reminisce on the flight up from D.C. After I left for college, my parents had moved to Saratoga, and I didn't have much of a reason to go back to Riverbend. I did my undergraduate degree at Dartmouth and decided that law school was a better option than looking for a job with a degree in philosophy. I had a few options but decided to go to Georgetown. That turned out to be an exceptional decision. Not only did I graduate as the valedictorian, I found the love of my life, Sally Gibb.

We had only that one date in Riverbend, but it stayed with both of us. Oh, we had both done our share of going out with other people, but we never seemed to find the right one. Then we found ourselves sitting next to each other in our Contracts class, and I had that same "banana oil" feeling I knew from the bowling alley. She was always the right one. Just took a while for it to sink in. I often wondered how we both managed to find ourselves at the same law school in the same class. It was definitely some good karma somewhere. We started dating again, and after graduation, we got married. We both agreed we wanted to stay in the D.C. area. Sally went to work for the State Department, ingratiating herself to Secretaries from both parties and eventually becoming undersecretary for Asia. I clerked for a federal judge, spent some years with one of the big name law firms, and decided to run for Congress from the Maryland district we lived in. That had been my job for the last twenty years.

Riverbend continued to deteriorate under a succession of mayors who rarely had any government experience, much less management experience. Most of the east end where I lived had become tenement-like and was now primarily home to immigrants, mostly from Puerto Rico, who came to work in the few factories that were left. Taxes became astronomical while home prices were dropping steadily. The mansions built by the old factory owners, bankers, and businessmen could be bought at fire sale prices, as long as someone didn't mind paying $10,000 in taxes for a 4,000 square foot house that might sell for $70,000. They estimated 1,700 houses were vacant, some so dilapidated the city simply knocked them down. You could drive down almost any street in Riverbend and see a hole where a house used to stand.

The downtown mall eventually did get built, as did the new bridge, and a maze of roads that effectively isolated one part of the city from another. Whatever character there was died in a desperate attempt to resuscitate the city. It turned out that the cure was worse than the disease. The first year the mall was open, all the spaces were filled, but over time, people started shopping at the big box stores that had been built just beyond the city limits. Eventually, the mall became mainly an indoor walking area for senior citizens, although there was an occasional government office that took advantage of the cheap rent.

The mall inevitably destroyed the downtown. Riverbend was never going to be like Cooperstown, with a downtown that had an 1800s quaintness about it, but with a little sprucing up, it could have functioned as a tourist stop for people on their way to the Sacandaga Lake or who didn't want to pay Saratoga prices for lodging in August. It was actually closer to New York City than Saratoga. Instead, the mall turned out to be the city's headstone. Riverbend simply couldn't embrace the idea that they could be something other than a gritty, workingman's berg, with factories and bars driving the economy. I thought perhaps over the entrance to the closed mall, they could have written the epitaph of Riverbend: They just didn't know any better.

The city compounded its mistakes by selling water to all the retail development in the area just outside the city limits, when they should have made the water supply contingent upon the stores annexing into the city. The reason was the same reason everything happened in Riverbend. The people with the money weren't going to let the amateur politicians cost them one extra dollar on their development. Agreements were made, legal documents were signed, and nobody knew enough or cared enough to protest. Millions in revenues bypassed Riverbend, leaving the city in worse shape than during the David Greene administration.

At least the golf course was still popular. There were a few more patches of crabgrass in the fairways than when Tony Gallo was taking care of it, but it was still like a private country club for Riverbend's golfers.

I shook my head. It was as pretty a valley as God could have created, a setting that would be impossible to find again, and greed and incompetence turned it into a place you only wanted to be from. In forty years, my high school class had never had a reunion. I assumed it was because there was almost no one left in Riverbend to organize it. The population left in the City of Riverbend was at best fifteen thousand people. It wasn't even large enough to be a city anymore. The city was full of unemployed people on public assistance and old people who had lived there all their lives. The population number was only destined to decrease.

Vinnie met me at baggage claim. "Capital city of one of the biggest states in the country, but it's still kind of a quaint airport," he said. "Sally couldn't make it?"

"Diplomatic mission to Asia with the president. Can't say no to the big guy."

"Too bad. I was looking forward to seeing her. How's the Congressman business?"

I said, "We make Tony Gallo and his gang look positively competent compared to us. Don't get me started. The only thing worse than the stupid things that make the paper are the stupid things some of them say in private. How's the heart surgery business."

"You know. Everybody needs a good plumber. I do more balloons than a clown at a kid's party. My father always wanted me to make a living with my hands. Beats the hell out of digging ditches though. C'mon, I'll take you to Casa di Vinnie."

I said, "Anybody home at the moment?"

"No," Vinnie said. "I'm working on finding ex-wife number three. Cindy, my oldest, is working in New York as a fashion designer. Melissa is teaching third grade in Glens Falls. How about your kids?"

"They're all doing great. Emma just graduated from NYU, and she'll be starting graduate school at Columbia in the fall. Ethan is on Wall Street. Erin is interning at State, and Elijah is writing for the *Post*. I'm pretty sure I'm past the point where I'm going to get that call in the middle of the night from the cops, 'Mr. Petrosino, we have your kid down at the station.' You can't ask for more than kids who are doing well."

We walked to Vinnie's car. "This your kid's car?" I said. "A 280Z?"

"Always wanted one. It's my baby."

We got in the car. "It's good to see you again, Vinnie," I said.

"It's good to see you too, G. Been way too long."

On the ride home, we talked about some of the people we knew. As long as it had been since we had seen each other, we fell into the conversation like it was yesterday. We got to Vinnie's house in half an hour.

"Want something to eat, G?"

"No, actually I'd love a Sambuca. Neat."

"That sounds good. I think I'll join you."

Vinnie poured the drinks and sat down. "Why do you think Mingo did it, G? I mean if there was anyone in the world you'd have expected to do anything to win it was Mingo."

"I actually don't think Mingo intended to stand up the way he did. I think right before he threw that last ball he decided that knowing he won because Peckham threw the match was something that would have bothered him forever. I think he knew he was going to foul, I'd catch him, and he could join the rest of the crowd in protesting, figuring eventually the match would have to go to Peckham. Mingo had a huge ego for a guy that wasn't good at anything other than bowling, and maybe it was his ego that didn't let him win that way. I think he really believed he was better than Peckham, and he wanted to win straight up. When he saw the crowd wasn't going to go along with the foul call, maybe he just decided that one time in his life he was going to do the right thing. I'll say this. In twenty years in Congress, I've never seen a colleague be that kind of standup guy, especially when he had everything to lose. Whatever you want to say about Mingo, he did something most of us would have never had the courage to do."

Vinnie said, "Did you think about not calling the foul? As much as we disliked Mingo, beating Peckham was a big deal for Riverbend."

"It was funny. I didn't have time to think about it. I saw his foot go over, and I raised my hand," I said. "But I remember watching Mingo setting up, and I knew he was ahead of his normal spot. Not by much. Just enough for his toes to go over the line. He knew what he was doing."

Vinnie said, "He still tried to make it as a pro, but Peckham had him blacklisted. Unfortunately for Peckham, what little good will he had left with his fellow pros evaporated when it came out he tried to throw the match for money. Peckham kept insisting he couldn't go through with throwing the match because he couldn't stand the idea of Mingo knocking him off the top of the heap. Swore that split was legitimate. Mingo went back to working at the supermarket, inherited the place when his father died, but couldn't compete against the big stores. When he died, he was selling used cars and doing cheesy TV commercials for a dealer named Perillo. Never left Riverbend though."

"The cops bursting in shocked everyone," Vinnie said. "As soon as they announced themselves, everybody stampeded for the door. They were yelling for everyone to freeze, but they were helpless against the crowd. They managed to grab Mayor Greene who was yelling, 'You've got the wrong guy. You want the fat guy.' They also snagged Giuseppe Simone. That turned out to be bad news for Tony Gallo, since he'd never have been there except for Tony."

I said, "Yeah, they all got what was coming to them. Tony had been stealing for decades. When they finally found his bank accounts, he had over ten million stuffed away. Had to give it all back. He figured he wasn't going to avoid jail, but he needed to avoid Giuseppe Simone, so he turned state's witness. Apparently, he knew things about Simone's operation and had actually been kicking funds to him. Gave up Stan Braxton too. Turns out, all that road and bridge money didn't find its way to just roads and bridges. Before Braxton got convicted, he managed to get elected again. He may have been a crook, but he was Riverbend's crook. Tony got witness relocation, but it isn't easy to hide a six-foot-three, 350-pound man with a gap between his teeth the size of the Holland Tunnel. Rumor was that Giuseppe's guys eventually found him in Salmon, Idaho, five years later. Tony couldn't stand the food in Idaho and decided to open his own Italian restaurant. One day, Tony didn't show up for work. The best that they could piece together was that a couple of strangers had eaten at the restaurant the day before he disappeared. Who knows for sure. Maybe Tony saw the wise guys and managed to disappear on his own. He was a resourceful guy after all."

Vinnie said, "You ever run into Borneo or Albert?"

"Borneo and I had lunch last week. Nobody calls him Borneo anymore. In fact, I'm the only one allowed to. To everyone else, it's Bruno or Mr. Rocca. After all, he's the founder and the executive director of the Association of Combat Veterans, biggest veterans' group in the country. Vets from WWII to Korea to Vietnam to Iraq and Afghanistan. He's a passionate lobbyist, and he is still my good friend. He's impossible to say no to. Still looks tough as nails, older but in great shape. Borneo kept Albert with him until he passed away. Years of hard drinking and living outdoors took its toll. He had a liver transplant but died a month later. I visited him in the hospital after the transplant operation. He said, 'I don't think I ever thanked you properly for saving my life.' I said, 'What do you mean? You saved Borneo's life.' Albert shook his head. 'No, I was the one who jumped in. I decided I was going to swim out into the river until one of the currents sucked me under or I just gave out. I thought I was tired of living. Borneo jumped in after me, even though he couldn't swim. He tried splashing out to where I was swimming but got caught in the current and started moving downstream. I heard him yell, turned back, and saw him struggling to stay up. That's when you saw me swimming toward him. It was fine if I died, but Borneo didn't have to die too.'

"I never did quite understand how Borneo got in the water. That explained it. We couldn't bury him with military honors, but he helped so many veterans, so many people who were as broken as he was. Guys turning to drugs and drinking to ease whatever their pain was. Albert was there for them no matter what time of the day or night they called. When they held the funeral, the church was filled with uniformed guys. In his own way, he served his country and supported his brothers. I was there with Borneo on Albert's last day. He died happy, and he died as good and as selfless a soldier as anyone had ever been."

Vinnie said, "I'm happy to hear that."

"I wonder why Frank never reopened the bowling alley after the big match?" I asked.

"Hard to say. He was losing all his pin boys. The match was a total bust. Riverbend was pretty much a laughingstock before that, more so after that. That bowling alley wasn't a moneymaker anyway. For a guy who lived as unhealthy a life as Frank did, he surprised everyone. Died in '95. I saw the obituary and went to the funeral. There were only five people there, one was his kid. Who knew Frank was a father. The alleys became as dilapidated as most of the town. Somebody tried to make it a historic building, but it was just old. They finally tore it down. You'd never know it had been there if you walked past the spot today."

I said, "Paulie DiMeo came out of that better than anyone. He declared the match no contest, most of the people just got their money back. But without Tony's protection, the state cops hounded him out of business. Well, that and the fact that the state decided betting the number was only a crime if someone other than the government was running it. The real 'outfit' muscled out the old outfit. Off track betting took care of the horseracing part of his book. He pretty much had nothing left but sports betting, and you didn't need a storefront for that."

Vinnie said, "Yeah, Peckham and his manager got nothing. They tried to sneak out of town that night, but the state patrol stopped Di Felipo's Cadillac on the Thruway near Syracuse. They both refused to testify about anything, but with Tony turning, they didn't need them. Like I said, Peckham stayed on top of the bowling world for a while, but the troubles he had with his fellow pros and the stain of that match was too much. He wasn't the same guy after the match with Mingo. He retired in his prime, eventually went back to Buffalo and bought himself a cheap strip club on Bailey Avenue."

"I heard Danny passed a while back," I said.

"Yeah. It was sad. His mom had taken care of him until she died. He was devoted to her just like she was to him. He worked the whole time. Bagging groceries and shagging carts at the supermarket. They loved him up there. Remember he used to live on Patriot Street, not more than two blocks from the bowling alley? They both were devastated when they had to move. They took that whole block for the mall. Neither of them did well after that. Once Danny's mom passed, there wasn't any other relative he could move in with, and they made Danny move to a home for the mentally challenged. Couldn't go to work anymore. He just withered away. G, you want to do something good for the world, find a way to make sure that people like Danny have a way to have a good life instead of being shuttered away from the rest of the world."

I nodded. Danny was a good man, a good coworker. I'd make it a point to honor his memory. Between Danny and Borneo I had a lot of work to do in Congress.

"What ever happened to Crackers?" I asked.

"You kidding? He started a travel agency. He's got twenty different locations all over the Capital District. And you should see him. Lost enough weight that he looks like a matinee idol. He even does his own TV commercials. He specializes in tours to Italy. He always said he was going to travel. Figured out how to make a living at it."

I said, "I still feel sad about Riverbend. I can never say I liked it much growing up. I certainly couldn't wait to get out of there. Once I left, I never really came back. Maybe it's more angry than sad. I think, if only crooks like Tony Gallo got cleaned out before they had infected everything in the town. If only someone knew how to stand up to the greedy *stronzos* who had all the money and were calling all the shots. If only there were professional people running the government instead of political hacks. It could have been the jewel of the Mohawk."

Vinnie said, "I don't know. The people supported the mall. It sounded like a great idea until a few years after they built it. Maybe with the right management, they can become a great town again."

Vinnie poured two more Sambucas. "*Salud*, my old friend. Here's to pin boys and Riverbend and Mingo."

The next morning, we drove down the Thruway to Riverbend. We walked inside of Most Precious Blood Church. It hadn't changed in forty years. The diocese built it as a one-third scale model of St. Patrick's in New York City, and it was still as nice a church as any parish without a cathedral had. Vinny and I looked for the family. Mingo's siblings and their families were there, various aunts and uncles and cousins. I introduced myself to many of them, expressed my condolences, and thanked them for the opportunity to speak. The bell in the sacristy rang, the priest came out flanked by two altar boys, and the funeral mass began. At the appropriate spot, the priest called me to the podium.

"Marcus Aurelius Pandolfo, the man everyone called Mingo, may have been the most courageous person I ever knew. Let me tell you why. Everybody remembers his first job. Mine was a pin boy at Riverbend Alleys, Riverbend, New York. It was 1968, and I was thirteen years old…"

ABOUT THE AUTHOR

Rich Halvey has written hundreds of articles on horseracing, environmental, and energy issues. After seeing a picture of some pin boys in a newspaper, he thought it would be a unique subject for a book. This is his second book and his first attempt at fiction. He's currently retired and writing, golfing, and riding horses.

CPSIA information can be obtained
at www.ICGtesting.com
Printed in the USA
FSHW010630290920
74220FS